SHERLOCK HOLMES
MYSTERY MAGAZINE

VOL. 6, NO. 6   **Issue #21**

FEATURES

NON FICTION

FICTION

CLASSIC REPRINT

ART & CARTOONS

" AS A PROFESSOR, MORIARTY, I'VE ALWAYS WANTED
TO KNOW, DO YOU GIVE A LOT OF HOMEWORK? "

STAFF

Publisher: John Betancourt
Editor: Marvin Kaye
Non-fiction Editor: Carla Coupe
Assistant Editor: Steve Coupe

Sherlock Holmes Mystery Magazine is published by Wildside Press, LLC. Single copies: $10.00 + $3.00 postage. U.S. subscriptions: $59.95 (postage paid) for the next 6 issues in the U.S.A., from: Wildside Press LLC, Subscription Dept. 9710 Traville Gateway Dr., #234; Rockville MD 20850. International subscriptions: see our web site at www.wildsidepress.com. Available as an ebook through all major ebook etailers, or our web site, www.wildsidepress.com.

COMING NEXT TIME...

STORIES! ARTICLES!
SHERLOCK HOLMES & DR. WATSON!

Sherlock Holmes Mystery Magazine #22
is just a few months away...watch for it!

Not a subscriber yet?
Send $59.95 for 6 issues (postage paid in the U.S.) to:

Wildside Press LLC
Attn: Subscription Dept.
9710 Traville Gateway Dr. #234
Rockville MD 20850

You can also subscribe online at
www.wildsidepress.com

FROM WATSON'S NOTEBOOKS

This issue of *Sherlock Holmes Mystery Magazine* introduces America's most famous consulting detective Nero Wolfe, who lives and works in Manhattan on West 35th Street with his colleague and scribe Archie Goodwin. Further details appear below in Mr Kaye's portion of our foreword to the reader. As some of you may be aware, considerable speculation was begun many years ago when in his massive tome *The Annotated Sherlock Holmes*, William S. Baring-Gould suggested that Holmes and Wolfe are related by blood. I have been asked about this many times, but regretfully cannot comment for legal reasons as well as Holmes's desire never to discuss it. I am told that Mr. Goodwin also has been instructed to maintain silence on this issue.

And now here is my fellow editor Mr Kaye.

–John H Watson, M D

⤬　⤬　⤬　⤬

A word is in order concerning the first new Nero Wolfe short story in many years, "A Tight Fit." As a member of The Wolfe Pack, which celebrates America's largest detective, I was at the annual Black Orchid Banquet when members were asked which author should continue the series now that Rex Stout was gone. Three names were put forward: Robert Parker, Lawrence Block and myself. But the only story I wanted to tell was how Wolfe first met Archie Goodwin—however, this has been done too well to repeat the effort, first by Robert Goldsborough, whose Nero Wolfe novels are well worth reading. The other origin story, "Firecrackers," appeared in The Wolfe Pack's magazine under a pseudonym, but was written by the late Henry Enberg, who also penned two excellent Wolfean radio plays. Thanks to the Pack's Werowance (President) Ira Matetsky, all three of Henry's works will appear in upcoming issues of *Sherlock Holmes Mystery Magazine*.

The idea for "A Tight Fit" occurred to me, as well as other new NW adventures. Thanks to the Rex Stout Estate managed by his two daughters Barbara Stout and Rebecca Stout Bradbury, I have been granted permission to offer them in this and future issues. For those of you not familiar with the Nero Wolfe Corpus (and shame on you!), Bob Goldsborough has assembled a roster of Nero Wolfe's so-called West 35th Street Irregulars.

✗ ✗ ✗ ✗

Wildside Press, publisher of *Sherlock Holmes Mystery Magazine*, has informed me that each issue is losing money and will therefore be terminated after #25. However, I have proposed to work out careful budgets and reduce the length of each issue in hopes of continuing. John Betancourt, head of Wildside Press, says that if he at least breaks even, he will see that *SHMM* continues.

The contents, therefore, of the next several issues may need to be revised and for this I hope our contributors will remain patient; I will be writing to all of them ASAP. At this stage *SHMM* 22 will include an article by Dan Andriacco about another of great detective, John Dickson Carr's Sir Henry Merrivale (H. M.).

Fiction will include Dr. Watson's "Adventure of the Cardboard Box," a new Nero Wolfe case, fiction by regulars Marc Bilgrey, contributing editor Eugene D. Goodwin, Laird Long, Stan Trybulski and others.

Canonically Yours,
Marvin Kaye
✗

ASK MRS HUDSON

by (Mrs) Martha Hudson

Dear Mrs Hudson,

I am puzzled and have been for quite some time as to the proper pronunciation for Mr Holmes's romantic ideal, Miss (formerly) Irene Adler, as well as Inspector Lestrade. And what is his first name?

Etymologically Curious

✗   ✗   ✗   ✗

Dear "Curious,"

Your puzzlement is quite understandable, but first let me dispossess you of that error that Mr Holmes harboured any feelings for Miss Adler other than respect for her ingenuity and resourcefulness. I know there are various theatrical and cinematic representations of Mr Holmes's cases that suggest he more than admired her. Indeed, Dr Watson exchanged some heated words with his literary agent, Sir Arthur Conan Doyle, for permitting that American thespian William Gillette to write a play about Mr Holmes that has him falling in love with—not Irene Adler—but a lady named Alice Faulkner.

By the way, it may surprise you to know that while she is mentioned in a few of Dr Watson's case histories, she only appears once—in "A Scandal in Bohemia"—and in that story, the good doctor makes it very clear to anyone capable of reading plain English that his friend never entertained any loving feelings for Miss Adler or anyone else!

Now both names that you inquire about are subjects of debate. Aficionados of Dr Watson's stories claim that Miss Adler's first name is pronounced the British way—Eye-REE-knee—but although I am not certain whether this is true, it is my belief that she was born in America in a state echoing part of our country: New Jersey. If that is so, then her name should be said as the Yanks do—Eye-REEN.

The inspector, who Dr Watson tells me was involved in at least thirteen of Mr Holmes's investigations, is now retired. I wrote to him asking about his surname, which I always heard said in the British manner—"Less-trade," and assumed it was just the Yanks who call him "Less-trahhd." Well, the answer is actually more complicated; he said that both pronunciations are correct because his forebears are both Cockney (Less-trade) and French (Less-trahhd).

I asked Dr Watson about the inspector's first name and, consulting his notes, he said that in his tale of "The Cardboard Box" he learned that Lestrade's first name begins with the letter G. In my letter, I asked him what the G. stood for, but he replied that he disliked his given name and preferred not to have it published. It was Mr Holmes who theorized that it obviously was an embarrassing subject for the inspector, and must stand for something strange or at least uncommon. Mr H suggests that it may be for Galahad, but that is only a guess.

Sincerely,
Mrs Hudson

✗   ✗   ✗   ✗

Dear Mrs Hudson,
Did you ever object to what Mr Holmes calls his "Baker Street Irregulars?"
Thanks for your time,
Billy Chaplin

✗   ✗   ✗   ✗

Dear Billy,
Come now! Did you think I wouldn't recognize you as my good tenant's chief of the Irregulars?! Of course, that was clever of you employing the surname of that great comedian Charlie Chaplin. (I mentioned it to Mr Holmes, who did not know the significance, but Dr Watson did, as he attended the performance of the above-mentioned play, *Sherlock Holmes*, by Mr Gillette, who employed young Charlie onstage as Billy, that is, yourself.)

But I don't mind your question. It was only the first time when you and the other rag-tags showed up in my B apartment that irritated me because your collective shoes tracked mud on the staircase and carpet. But Mr Holmes settled it to my satisfaction by instructing all future visits to be made solely by you, and only after you'd brushed your shoes before entering. (Somehow this event, which I don't think Dr W wrote up, appears in one of the first films made with Mr Rathbone and Mr Bruce.)

Fondly (and now I've embarrassed you!),
Mrs H

✗ ✗ ✗ ✗

Dear Mrs Hudson,

I wonder whether Mr Holmes and Dr Watson have seen any of the dramatic representations of their adventures, and if so, whom do they prefer portraying each other?

Yr Devoted Fan,
Leonard Newman

✗ ✗ ✗ ✗

Dear Mr Newman,

I am pleased that you have written to me. I have read your many film reviews and have enjoyed them, and I only have two minor quibbles:

1. At the close of the Rathbone version of "The Hound," you report him as saying, "Quick, Watson … the needle!" This phrase, which I am sure Mr Holmes *never said*, was, in that film, just "Watson … the needle."

2. You call twelve of the Universal Studios motion pictures up-datings, but that does not quite apply to *Sherlock Holmes Faces Death*, which is based on "The Musgrave Ritual." True, there are some British military veterans in the story, but otherwise the film looks like one of the most atmospheric "period" pieces in the group, and one might argue likewise for *The Scarlet Claw* and *The Pearl of Death*, and at least one more, *The House of Fear*, which Dr Watson likes because it is he who solves it even before Mr Holmes!

At any rate, anyone who looks at these films today must regard them, by now, as period pieces.

Now to your question. It is easy enough to name Dr Watson's preferences, for he only told me of six that he saw and he has no objections to any of them, although he is sorry that Nigel Bruce was made to—as the Yanks put it—"dumb down" his portrayal in the later movies, though he is not at all bumbling in the first six, and he is so dear throughout that his namesake does not mind. Dr W also liked the versions of himself played by Donald Houston, Nigel Stock, H. Marion Crawford, and André Morrell, though he says the latter "just doesn't have the right look." His personal favourite, though, is James Mason in *Murder By Decree*, which, says my tenant, "has nothing to do with reality."

It's more complicated, though, when we turn to Mr Holmes, and that is partly because he has seen no fewer than eleven different Holmes impersonators, so to speak. He never saw Mr Gillette's original four-act drama because Dr Watson warned him of its "love interest," but he did attend a performance of Gillette's one-act play, *The Peculiar Predicament of Sherlock Holmes*, and found it amusing. (The predicament is that he never gets any chance to speak!) Of the ten remaining actors, Mr Holmes only dislikes two: Christopher Plummer in *Murder By Decree*, "who wears his heart on his sleeve, which I hope I never do," and Jeremy Brett, who positively infuriates The Great Detective. "Had I behaved as rudely as he did when entering the homes of British royalty, I would have promptly been shown the door, and that forcefully." But in fairness to Mr Brett, Dr Watson rather likes his Holmesian television series. To begin with, he saw and enjoyed Mr Brett in an early production on "the tube" of *The Merchant of Venice*, in which he played Bassanio opposite Sir Laurence Olivier as Shylock (which I thought an odd bit of casting) and Joan Plowright as Portia. The doctor's admiration of the Brett programmes is based on two points; first, he considers them fairly faithful to his written stories, and second, he likes both of the actors who played Dr W, David Burke and Edward Hardwicke.

Returning to Mr Holmes, of the remaining actors, he liked John Barrymore (odd that his name is shared by the butler of Baskerville Hall), Frank Langella, John Neville, and Arthur Wontner. His four favourite Sherlock Holmes portrayals are, in ascending order, Ronald Howard, Christopher Lee, Peter Cushing, and (his all-time favourite) Basil Rathbone.

Sincerely,
Mrs Hudson

✗ ✗ ✗ ✗

Dear Mrs Hudson,

I hope you shall not think it indelicate of me to ask how it is possible that you, Mr Holmes, Dr Watson, and Inspector Lestrade are still alive after such a very very very long time?!

Apologies,

Robert N Shaw

⤬   ⤬   ⤬   ⤬

Dear Mr Shaw,

No apologies required … though all of us are retired, your curiosity is well-founded. We live separately, me as house-keeper with light duties with Mr Holmes, while Lestrade and Dr Watson are in London, where Dr W manages 221 Baker Street for me.

For a time, neither Mr Holmes nor Dr Watson cared to talk about this, but they have now given me permission to reveal the source of our longevity. It is two-fold.

Mr Holmes is a pioneer in a branch of science now called cryogenics, and he it was who theorized that one might be frozen and stored at the moment of death, so that biological decay would not occur, there to remain till science had advanced to a point where it could revive the dormant person and cure whatever "did 'im in." After that, he designed an actual unit in which each of us could be cryogenically stored. I admit that I was chary of such a proceeding, but when I grew quite ill, Dr W persuaded me to allow it, and I did.

Now that we are all returned, Mr Holmes has us take three kinds of medicines twice daily. The first is HGH, or Human Growth Hormone, which begins to taper off as we grow older, and by this we lose our youthful resilience and show the signs of aging. HGH replaces our own supply. The second substance is an amino acid compound, which stimulates the body to make its own natural HGH, and finally, we take something called Somastatin, which fights the body's attempt to throw off the benefits of HGH. These products are now orderable online at various sites; the ones Mr Holmes and the rest of us use is www.antiagingresearch.com.

You may wish to try these items.

In Good Health,

Mrs Hudson

⤬   ⤬   ⤬   ⤬

I present below a light dinner for warmer weather.

COLD TOMATO SOUP

3 cups of cubed tomatoes without their skins or centers
2 cups of diced onions
2 cups of cubed cucumbers without their skins or centers
3 basil leaves
1 teaspoon of diced mint
2 cups of chicken broth
2 cups of yogurt
2 tablespoons of butter
Salt, to taste

1. Melt the butter in a frying pan.
2. Put in the onion.
3. Cook for ten minutes, stirring the mixture all the time.
4. Add the cucumber, tomatoes, basil and chicken broth.
5. Cook for half-an-hour, stirring the mixture frequently.
6. Strain the mixture through a sieve, or use an electric blender.
7. Pour it into a bowl.
8. Add the yogurt and salt.
9. Chill the mixture.
10. Just before serving it, add the mint.

✗   ✗   ✗   ✗

SWEET AND SOUR BRISKET

3 pounds of brisket of beef
1 onion slice
1 serving of lemon juice
1 bay leaf
3 tablespoons of sugar
Dill, to taste
Salt and pepper, to taste

1. Place the meat in a large pot.
2. Add bay leaf, onion, pepper and salt.
3. Pour in a cup of boiling water.
4. Simmer for 2 ½ hours.
5. Add lemon juice and sugar till the meat becomes sweet and sour, to taste.

⨯　⨯　⨯　⨯

GREEN BEANS IN SOUR CREAM

A quantity of cooked and drained French green beans, as required.
1/3 cup of diced onions
¾ cups of any grated sharp cheese
1 cup of sour cream
1 tablespoons of flour
1 tablespoon of butter
1 tablespoon of salt
¼ teaspoon of pepper

1. Fry onions in butter.
2. Add the sour cream to the onions.
3. Put in the flour, salt and pepper.
4. Simmer it all.
5. Put the beans in a 1 ½ quart baking dish.
6. Put in the sour cream, etc., and mix thoroughly.
7. Put the cheese on top.
8. Cover it and bake at 350 degrees for a quarter-hour.

⨯　⨯　⨯　⨯

DRUNKEN CORN ON THE COB

New corn cobs, as many as are required
¼ pound of butter per cob
Salt
Pale ale, one bottle for two cobs

1. Place the corn cobs on a sheet of aluminium foil.
2. Bake the corn in the oven at 325 degrees for 15 minutes or less (check on progress!).
3. Remove the corn and place in a large pot.
4. Salt the corn, turning each cob till all of it is covered.
5. Add the pale ale.
6. Slowly simmer the corn until the ale is reduced by approximately half.
7. Serve the corn with the butter on the side.
8. Pour the remaining ale into a spouted container for additional basting by the diners.

✗ ✗ ✗ ✗

SHERRY AND CREAM DESSERT

¾ of a cup of sweet sherry wine
¼ cup of lemon juice
Grated rind from two lemons
½ cup of sugar
1 ½ cups of thick cream
1/8 teaspoon of nutmeg

1. Place the sugar, lemon rind and the juice in a small bowl.
2. Use a whisk on this mixture until the sugar dissolves.
3. Add the sherry and whisk the mixture.
4. Add the cream and nutmeg and whisk till the mix has body.
5. Add the sherry mixture to the cream and nutmeg and whisk it all once more.

✗

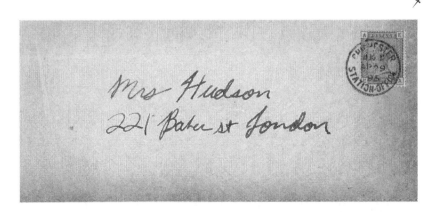

SCREEN OF THE CRIME

by Kim Newman

In 2013, writer-director Andrey Kavan made a *Sherlok Kholms* series for Russian television, consisting of six feature-length episodes. It has turned up on youtube with fan-made sub-titles. Its approach to the Conan Doyle source material might once have been considered radical, though now it's almost a default to throw away the deerstalker and the meticulous unflappability to present a stubbled, slovenly bipolar Holmes and a PST-suffering Watson pitted against a chaotic, corrupt world with much contemporary resonance. If you think the BBC's current *Sherlock* is overshadowed by its Watson's hard times in a more recent Afghan war than the one Doyle wrote about, imagine how Russians feel about that blood-soaked patch of the world map. Unlike *Sherlock* and *Elementary*, *Sherlok Kholms* doesn't relocate the characters to a contemporary setting—but it goes further than Guy Ritchie's films in finding Victorian parallels for the way things are today.

In 1979, then-Soviet television produced a fond (and fondly-remembered) *Adventures of Sherlock Holmes and Doctor Watson* with Vasily Livanov and Vitaly Solomin as a genial sleuth and his intrepid sidekick. *Sherlok Kholms* positions itself as radically different from this show, but is structurally rather close to it—with miniseries-like overall arcs to do with the developing relationship of Holmes and Watson and the shadow of Moriarty, and key stories pulled out of canonical order and slotted in to highlight the lead characters. The older show presented its heroes in a nostalgic light—expressing a peculiarly Russian anglophilia—and stressed comradeship and noble endeavour, but the new take is complicated and sometimes uncomfortable. A sub-plot has Watson (Andrey Panin) struggling to become a writer, debating with a publisher about how to make his accounts of thorny real stories more saleable. This suggests that the versions we're familiar with are removed from a truth we are only now being let in on. Throughout, characters say or do things this Watson could never put in print—Watson's marriage proposal to Mrs Hudson (Ingeborna Dapkunaite) is astonishing enough without the throw-away revelation (unthinkable in any British or American Doyle adaptation) that much of the doctor's struggling practice involves performing "underground abortions." The approach has some tex-tural precedent in that Doyle has Holmes complain about the way Watson dramatises their cases, but this goes further even than *The Private Life of Sherlock Holmes* or *Mr Holmes* in making its takes on Doyle's characters vastly different from the ones found on the page. There's a sustained riff on the adverse reactions of the people involved when Watson's stories see print: Mrs Hudson resents be-ing represented as "an old granny" and gives him till the end of the month to get out of 221B …

The first episode, *Beyker Strit, 221B* (*Baker Street 221B*), opens with exactly the quotation about the Afghan War from *A Study in Scarlet* used in *The Abominable Bride* ("the campaign brought honours and promotion to many but for me it had nothing but mis-fortune and disaster") as Watson returns to London, "health irrepa-rably damaged," and is drawn into an alliance with Holmes. In an unusual selection, their first case is "Black Peter," with Aleksandr Ilin as a suitably imposing, impaled dastard. In suitably dramatic fashion, Watson meets Holmes (Igor Petrenko) over a corpse ly-ing in the street and wind up in separate quarters at 221B. This Watson is balding, moustached and more affected psychologically than physically by the war—and Panin, who narrates and frames each episode scratching away with his pen, is the lead actor here. Petrenko's Holmes looks and acts more like a revolutionary poet than a detective: unshaven, fiddling with rimless glasses, getting drunk rather than taking drugs, treated pretty much as a criminal busybody by the police and flattened in his first "boxing lesson" with Watson. A very Russian take on male bonding involves hard liquour, pugilism and tears. There's a running joke as Watson as-sumes several fussy little old ladies in and around Baker Street are his new landlady … only for the slim, glamorous Dapkunaite to show up at the end (the biggest star in the show, the Lithuanian actress was in *Burnt By the Sun* and has English language credits in *Mission: Impossible*, *Shadow of the Vampire*, *Prime Suspect* and *Wallander*) and strike sparks with the retiring doctor.

Kamen, Nozhnitsy, Bumaga (*Rock, Paper, Scissors*) is a loose adaptation of *The Sign of Four*, which quickly manages to introduce Irene Adler (a lively, lissom Lyanka Gryu), Mycroft (whose face isn't shown—setting up a payoff we have to wait six episodes for) and the malign influence of Moriarty. Here, Watson is involved in the backstory of the Agra treasure as a comrade of the guilty officers—who have returned to London and become a criminal gang, working as cabdrivers to expedite burglaries. Holmes is drawn into the case when Peter Small (Mikhail Evlanov), an old comrade of Watson's, shows up in Baker Street badly wounded, taking advantage of the special rates Watson offers for veterans. In the finale, the detective is shut out of a duel at an officers's club between a grim Watson and virulent racist Thad Sholto (Igor Skylar). Your assumptions about the politics of Russian popular entertainment might well be challenged by the way the villain of the piece spouts anti-immigrant/refugee sentiments which sound horribly familiar in the 21ˢᵗ century … and is roundly condemned for it. The scene has added bite in that several of the extras are visibly and genuinely scarred—are they real veterans of the USSR's Afghan campaign? In a later episode, Watson's publisher tells him to drop the "chauvinist officer" and the politics and invent a romance to dress up the story. Here, Mary (Elizaveta Alekseeva) is Small's orphan daughter and it's Holmes who sends her an annual pearl (for her board and education) from the otherwise lost treasure; we're to infer that Watson spins this into the love story of *The Sign of Four*, and that the imaginary romance is another thing that irritates Mrs Hudson about Watson's writing.

Only in *Payatsy* (*Clowns*) does the focus start to shift from Watson to Holmes. A key clue in the previous episode is a photograph of the guilty officers taken in Afghanistan, with a shadowy physics professor nearly cropped out. A great deal of time is spent trying to get a full version of the photo as Holmes begins to perceive a single hand behind most of the evil in London. It is personal for the detective in that Irene, who keeps showing up briefly to overturn his composure, is ensnared in the coils of Moriarty. This episode has a magnificently gruesome opening as a wedding photographer is murdered when his flash powder is replaced with TNT, spattering the bride (Natalya Turkina) with gore. The story then revolves around farcical diplomatic business about a fake affair between the

American ambassador's naïve wife and a French diplomat which might foment a war between France and America. In a splendid bit of new Holmesianism, the bride is too shocked to describe Moriarty, whom she has seen, and the detective seizes on her profession (fishmonger) to cajole her to think in piscine terms and liken the villain to a pike (long face), crab (eyestalk-like blue spectacles) and an octopus (tentacular arms). This Holmes is anything but immune to emotion—he slaps Watson for calling Irene a whore, and rolls around on the floor in agony when betrayed yet again.

Lyubovnitsy Lord Maulbreya (*The Mistress of Lord Maulbrey*), a case made from whole cloth, features an apparent serial murderer who is eliminating the women who might be mentioned in the will of a wealthy, just-dead aristocrat. It offers a solid, formidable villain in Gilbert Roy (Leonid Timtsunik), who is shockingly violent and ingenious (he favours a poison-dart-firing airgun disguised as a rolled newspaper), and an intriguing *femme fatale* in scheming innocent Ellen (Aleksandra Ursulyak), a gifted artist who presents Holmes with a sketch of the Professor he is looking for. We also learn that Moriarty (Aleksandr Adabashyan), aka Bernard Buckley, smokes distinctive Royal Caribbean cigars. Though Doyle set many stories in London and in rural areas, he oddly neglected to have Holmes work in any of the UK's other cities ... here, the case takes him and Lestrade (Mikhail Boyarskiy) to Bristol, where there's an impressive shoot-out in a hotel and on the street.

It's back to Doyle for the bones of a story in *Obrad Doma Meysgreyvov* (*The Musgrave Ritual*), a detour into the gothic which offers a snowbound Scots castle, a Baskerville-like naïve American Musgrave heir (Aleksandr Golubev), a dour bastard brother (Sergey Yushkevich) who insists even Holmes and Watson wear kilts in freezing weather, a centuries-old family feud, a black-robed ghostly monk (who might evoke Chekhov or Edgar Wallace), the sword of Charles I, Watson delirious with flu, and the arrival of the horseless carriage. The most traditional, standalone episode of the series, it might make a useful sampler for folks who just want to give the show a try—getting away from London for a spell means that Holmes and Watson are also away from their ongoing storylines. Suggesting that the makers have a familiarity with previous film and TV takes on the canon, the heir has the character name Reginald Owen, after one of the few actors to have played both Holmes and Watson.

By the time of *Gulifaks* (*Halifax*), Watson is a published author—and his work puts him on the outs with an offended Holmes and Mrs Hudson, while the resentful Lestrade is envious of how much the doctor is paid for his stories. With Holmes made famous, Baker Street is thronged with curiosity-seekers and Holmes worries he'll no longer be able to work anonymously. When a corrupt official is glimpsed in a deerstalker and checked cape, smoking a curved pipe, Holmes asks Watson to describe him as looking like that, to get back his ability to work undercover. This begins with a reasonably straight version of "The Red-Headed League," but the tunnel-to-the-bank business is just Act One of an insanely complex Moriarty plot to heist a printing press from the Royal Mint. The ruthlessness of all parties is stressed—Moriarty poisons the stooges he sends into the bank so they all die during a chase and policemen gun down suspects Wild West fashion. As in *Kamen, Nozhnitsy, Bumaga*, there's a theme about the pride of men in uniform. Lestrade (here, fully named as Fitzpatrick Lestrade) is coldly furious at the members of the police fraternity who have let down the side. Knowing that the constables who have muddy trousers have sold out to Moriarty, he lines his whole force up for inspection and walks past, calmly shooting the traitors. The eponymous Halifax (Andrey Merzlikin), a forger forced to work with the Moriarty gang, specialises in *trompe l'oeuil* tricks—painting a convincing escape tunnel entrance in a cell to alarm a warden—and seems to be making a philosophical point about how trapped and doomed everyone is.

Poslednee delo Kholmsa (*Holmes's Last Case*) opens with Irene in blackface singing "God Rest You Merry Gentlemen" at a Christmas entertainment at Brasher Castle, which is part of a jewel heist. The script takes a while to get to "The Final Problem," as it fills in the backstory of Holmes's relationship with Irene in a full-on Paris flashback which involves a meet cute at the base of the unfinished Eiffel Tower, a trip to the Moulin Rouge, absinthe-fuelled sex, impressionist art, and a mime. In the present, Watson and Martha Hudson finally stop bickering and he proposes; later, it seems they've become a couple, but not actually got married. The plot goes into full-on bizarre mode with an embassy robbery that exposes a mad science plan involving electrified steel needles which can turn ordinary men into zombic super-soldiers. The face-off in Switzerland features a frozen Reichenbach, much cheating as Moriarty brings a gun and a knife to a (brutal) martial arts fight, Holmes being canny enough to wear spiked shoes while his opponent slides around on the ice, and a noise-triggered avalanche which seems to do for both men—prompting Watson to write up a supposed last adventure even though there's one episode to go.

The finale is titled *Sobaka Baskervil* (*Baskerville Hound*), a canny piece of misdirection since the dog only turns up (in a new context) in the final scene, which features a visit to Baker Street by Queen Victoria (Svetlana Kryuchkova). It's three years since Watson wrote of Holmes's death, Professor Challenger is in London lecturing about evolution, and young war office clerk, Arthur Cadogan West, turns up dead in a fish tank in a market (with secret papers on his person) after falling from a train. On the assumption that he knows Holmes's methods, Watson is called in to investigate the crime (derived from "The Bruce-Partington Plans") in partnership with a nattily-dressed, bearded Mycroft, who turns out to be Sherlock's twin … with the not-dead detective at some point stepping in to impersonate his stuffier sibling to get back in the game. Panin enjoys the chance to play several takes on Sherlock and Mycroft, and the inevitable you're-not-dead shock reunions with the rest of the cast. Moriarty also survived the Reichenbach and—in a development rather like *Sherlock Holmes Game of Shadows*—a key player is cruelly sacrificed to remind us how evil he is. The mcguffin is an ingenious murder contraption wired to the clock of Big Ben (which is either great location work or very good CGI, for a finale reminiscent of the climax of the 1978 version of *The Thirty Nine Steps*). In a Scenes We'd Like to See moment, Holmes launches a furious tirade at the ingenious craftsman who's made the thing for the Professor without caring what he uses it for—remember Doyle's Holmes admiring the workmanship of Colonel Moran's airgun, which has been used in attempts to murder him.

Briefly, in this episode, Holmes puts on a deerstalker and a cape—only to complain that it's uncomfortable. But, by now, he's reconciled to being eclipsed by Watson's version of himself and touched at the title Watson chooses for his book of reminiscences, *My Friend Sherlock Holmes*. So, at the end, after all the reimagining, we come back to what is for this version—as for almost all other versions—the heart of the story, the comradeship of two admirable, difficult men in a world of crime, betrayal, love, honour, diabolic cunning, and basic decency.

✗

Kim Newman is a prolific, award-winning English writer and editor, who also acts, is a film critic, and a London broadcaster. Of his many novels and stories, one of the most famous is *Anno Dracula*.

BEAM ME UP, SHERLOCK!

SHERLOCK HOLMES & STAR TREK— A GALAXY OF SIMILARITIES

by Lynne Stephens

Any comparison between *Star Trek* and Sherlock Holmes must necessarily begin with an apology. The scope of these subjects extends over so many years, across so many "canons" and iterations and media, that to claim authoritative statements regarding every aspect of either narrative's footprint must be a fool's errand. Only the most dedicated mortal could consume it all, covering Arthur Conan Doyle's original Sherlock Holmes oeuvre: 56 short stories and four novels. Now let's add on the subsequent pastiches: 600+ released by for-profit publishers, and growing hourly, not to mention the hundreds of stage and screen adaptations and extensions. Need I drag out that old cocktail party one-liner about Sherlock Holmes being the most-represented character in the history of movies? Nah … you knew that one already.

Now let's switch over to catalog *Star Trek's* 79 original hours of televised "canon," expanded by four additional live-action series, augmented by the twelve movies, including the two J.J. Abrams films, then multiplied by over 650 novels, 500+ comic book issues, and numerous other authorized extensions.

And we haven't even given a nod yet to the additional galaxies of fanfiction for both these narratives, a truly mammoth realm encompassing tens of thousands of fan-created tales that have been passed around the pop cultural campfire from the days of small-edition printing to today's massive digital archives of fanfiction. net and AO3.

So any comparative survey, for sanity's sake alone, can cover only a personal scope to the limits of the surveyor's lifetime consumption.

Where to start? People like 'em both. Just sayin'. <cough> And they have, for a long time … 1887 for Holmes, 1966 for *Trek*.

And … when you look past the fog and the quatrotriticale, when you scrub away the hansom cabs and the tricorders and the villains of the week and all that … there's a great deal of similarity, both in the fictional worlds of the stories themselves, and also within our real universe, where creative minds have applied themselves to both the detective and the explorer, the biographer and the scientist, and the worlds enveloping both.

But back to defining scope and stickin' to it. For Holmes, I look to ACD's original canon, the lovely Granada series with Jeremy Brett, and the current BBC *Sherlock* series, as my orientation points, for no more justifiable reason than these are my personal faves. For *Star Trek*, there's the incomparable original series starring William Shatner and the late and lamented Leonard Nimoy, and I'll add in just a dab of the excellent follow-up series *Star Trek: The Next Generation*, with Patrick Stewart and Brent Spiner. Yes, yes, I know there were noble series that followed, but … none of them engaged my interest in the way the first two did. Television ratings in the USA support my preferences—no series after *ST:TNG* achieved a viewership higher than *ST:TNG* succeeded in achieving in its original run.

So … shall we begin?

Both *Star Trek* and Sherlock Holmes originated in eras of astounding scientific advancement and discovery. Both Arthur Conan Doyle and *Star Trek* creator Gene Roddenberry launched narratives with worldviews that trusted in morally-guided scientific knowledge to assist humans in accomplishing positive, or pro-social, outcomes. Both narratives never veer from an upbeat world view; no matter the crisis at hand, no matter how grim the scenario, cool heads and science-inspired reasoning will beat back chaos and inspire hope for the future.

Neither ACD nor Roddenberry approached life from the cosseting of an armchair. Both endured life-challenging experiences as young men, and both shifted to writing adventure-focused fiction on a full time-basis after working in another profession. While still a medical student, Conan Doyle faced down icy elements as the doctor on a whaling ship sent to the Arctic Circle. (ACD as McCoy, anyone?) ACD first put pen to paper in medical school and ultimately segued this interest into a full-time writing career after a relatively short and decidedly unremunerative medical career.

His Sherlock Holmes series stands as only one of many literary creations in a writing career that spanned beyond four decades. Conan Doyle's most popular characters aside from Holmes were also men of action: the Napoleonic-era Brigadier Gerard and *The Lost World's* Professor Challenger.

Roddenberry served in WWII, flying 89 missions with the Army Air Corps in the Pacific, and earned the Distinguished Flying Cross and an Air Medal in the process. While stationed in the Pacific he began to write short stories and poems. After the war he transferred his military skills to civilian use as a Pan Am pilot. He leveraged his communication skills into a career shift, becoming a Los Angeles Police Department spokesman, while selling TV screenplays on spec as a sideline for action series such as *Highway Patrol* and *Have Gun–Will Travel*. At the point where the gigs and money became relatively steady he quit law enforcement entirely to focus on a television writing career full time, creating and producing the series *The Lieutenant* before creating his space-set "wagon train to the stars" in 1964.

Both men married twice, and both became involved with the woman who would become their second wife while each was still married to his first. (Although I hear ACD indignantly assuring me that his relationship with Jean Leckie remained completely proper while Mary Louise remained alive.) Both had children from each of their marriages.

Roddenberry and ACD's lives included periods of physical challenge, and their stories featured plenty of rough-and-ready action, but there was also a spiritual questing in each man's nature. At the time of their deaths, both authors espoused a belief different than the one of their birth. While raised a Catholic, ACD's later-life association with Spiritualism is an oft-referenced chapter of his life, if for nothing else than the odd juxtaposition between the credulous fairy-loving author and his incredulous super-sleuth creation. Roddenberry grew up a Southern Baptist, but came to reject all organized religion and departed this life as a humanist.

ACD and Roddenberry's most memorable creations feature a sequence of stand-alone adventure tales with recurring characters. ACD, in fact, claimed that he invented the format of repeat characters in non-serialized tales to thwart the reasonable concern that the chapter-an-issue format, so successful for Charles Dickens earlier in the 19th century, would cumulatively lose readers over time if each issue wasn't assiduously purchased, and each chapter consumed in chronological sequence. ACD's format became the go-to template of most mid-century American television sitcoms and dramas for the same miss-one-and-you're-lost concern as ACD, only later, in the VCR era, returning to the early model of complex multi-season narratives arcs interwoven with episode-length crisis-of-the-week events. Both Holmes stories and *Star Trek* episodes often began and concluded "at home," amid the physical and psychological security of the fireside. Holmes's residence of 221B Baker Street boasted a literal fireside, corresponding to the figurative circular hearth of the Enterprise's bridge.

NBC cancelled *Star Trek* in 1969 after three years and 79 episodes. ACD pushed Holmes off the Reichenbach Falls in 1893, after complaining to his mother that "he takes my mind from better things." But like beloved zombies, these narratives refused to stay dead. The first semi-step to full-blown reincarnation for our consulting detective occurred when ACD published *The Hound of the Baskervilles* in 1901. While featuring the characters of Holmes and Watson, ACD side-stepped the question of full reincarnation by setting the story in a year earlier than that of "The Final Problem." (Holmes = Still Dead)

In 1972 *Star Trek* fans organized the first major *Star Trek* convention in NYC. They expected a modest turnout of like-minded individuals. What they got instead were 3,000 people descending on the Statler Hilton hotel, and an unplanned visit from the fire marshal. The Powers That Be took notice. The 1973-1974 animated *Star Trek* series, like *Baskerville*, served as the half-step towards full-blown resuscitation, testing the waters before green-lighting any more expensive outings.

ACD saw published his *coup de theatre mouille* in 1903, ten years after shoving the Master and Moriarty over the Swiss precipice. To his delighted readers he revealed the truth at last. (Holmes = Not Dead)

Star Trek: The Motion Picture premiered in 1979, also ten years since its ignoble cancellation, attracting a strong box office even without the burning question of a beloved character's survival. Fans didn't have to wait long, though. That plot point got trotted out within *Star Trek II: The Wrath of Khan* and *Star Trek III: The Search for Spock*. (Spock = It's Complicated)

These forays were merely the first of multiple, multiplying, and unending iterations, remakes, pastiches, parodies, and homages which continue to spring forth to this day, well after their original creators were respectfully laid to rest. (ACD/GR = Permanently Dead)

Why do both narratives continue to thrive? Leonard Nimoy summarized it well in a May 9, 1978 *Chicago Tribune* article:

> I think that people are still interested in 'Star Trek' for the same reasons they're still interested in Holmes. It presented a complete, credible world, just like Doyle's stories do. It didn't play down to viewers' intellects the way some of the space shows, like *Lost In Space* did; it wasn't played for fantasy. You had the bad guys and you had problems, but you also had dependable, incorruptible heroes to solve them. Real heroes. And boy, our society sure could use some of them today.

An additional connection between SH and *ST* is the sheer volume of artists who've had a hand in both worlds. Lovely Marina Sirtis played the key role of Deanna Troi in *ST:TNG*, but before that series began she was a guest artist in the Granada Holmes's teleplay of "The Six Napoleons." Both esteemed thespians Malcom McDowell and Christopher Plummer made their mark in both worlds: McDowell played Soran in *ST:Generations* and the voice of Moriarty in *Tom & Jerry Meet Sherlock Holmes*. Plummer played Chang in *STVI: The Undiscovered Country*, and Sherlock Holmes both in *Murder By Decree* and *Silver Blaze*. Dwight Schultz played dear old "Broccoli" in *ST:TNG*, and Daniel Davis played a much more sinister guest starring role (Moriarty) in the same series, but both men trod the boards in separate stage productions of "The Crucifer of Blood."

While William Shatner is obviously best known for his portrayal of James Tiberius Kirk in *Star Trek (The Original Series)*, he also played Stapleton in the 1972 TV movie *The Hound of the Baskervilles*, with Stuart Granger as Holmes and Bernard Fox as Watson. His *ST:TOS* costar, Leonard Nimoy, assayed Holmes on stage in the William Gillette play "Sherlock Holmes," in the mid 1970s. Of the detective, Nimoy said:

He's an asocial man, hardly your average 9 to 5 worker with a family. Instead, he's chosen a very special kind of life, and he has very little respect for most of the people around him who are also involved in his profession. He's an outsider, in so many ways—particularly in his relationships, or rather lack of relationships, with women. Holmes is very much an alien, all right, and I felt that I could understand him the same way I understood Spock. (*Chicago Tribune*, May 9, 1978)

Another high profile actor with a foot in both worlds is Benedict Cumberbatch, who plays the title character in *Sherlock* but also wowed audience and critics alike as the villain "John Harrison" in the second *ST:TOS* reboot franchise film, *Star Trek Into Darkness*. When hearing the assertion from "Harrison" that "I'm better than you." At what? "At … everything," it would be very easy to assume the line comes from Sherlock's mouth.

However, the single individual with perhaps the greatest overlap between the worlds of *ST* and SH is not a performer, but writer and director Nicholas Meyer. In the Holmes corner of the ring, we find Meyer as author of the highly regarded novel *The Seven-Per-Cent Solution*, as well as *The West End Horror*, and *The Canary Trainer*. Meyer also penned the script for the film adaption of *The Seven-Per-Cent Solution*. And on the *Star Trek* side of the ring, Meyer wrote (uncredited) and directed the beloved *Star Trek II: The Wrath of Khan*, wrote *Star Trek IV: The Voyage Home* (yes, the one with the whales), and wrote and directed *Star Trek VI: The Undiscovered Country*. The rare middle of the ring moment takes place in the third film, when Spock says, "An ancestor of mine maintained that if you eliminate the impossible, whatever remains, however improbable, must be the solution." The circle may be considered complete with the *Sherlock* episode "The Hounds of Baskerville," when John refers to Sherlock as "Spock."

An additional point of connectivity occurred in two episodes of *ST:TNG* that revolved around the character of Moriarty. While both stories are charming in their own right, the overarching conceit of the premise itself is highly satisfying: even in the 24th century, the stories and characters of ACD's Holmes are remembered and beloved. How this quite dovetails into the supposition that Holmes is a "real" person and Spock's ancestor, as per *Undiscovered Country*, given *TOS* and *TNG* exist in the same conceptual universe, doesn't quite hold up to scrutiny, but let's not dwell on that here ....

In the 1988 episode "Elementary, Dear Data" we first learn of the android Data's love for Sherlock Holmes stories. Data asks his friend Geordi to join him on the holodeck, a programmable virtual reality playground for the starship crew, to playact Sherlock Holmes stories as a relaxing activity, with Geordi pretending to be Watson. Unfortunately, once within the holodeck's Holmesian environment, Geordi soon gets frustrated and dissatisfied. Data can't cosplay for beans: he's dressed up as Holmes, and placed in the proper Victorian London setting, but being an android he's incapable of pretending that he's unaware of each story's denouement, so shortly after the mystery is constructed Data announces all the details of the "whodunit."

To fix the situation, Geordi rashly requests the Enterprise's computer to create an adversary that can defeat Data. The computer obliges by transforming one of the holodeck denizens of "Victorian London" into an increasingly sentient being who is aware that his name is "Moriarty" ... and quickly becomes aware of much more. Like Frankenstein's monster, Moriarty develops a nuanced awareness of self, and resolves to live beyond the confines of the holodeck. He kidnaps the ship's doctor, Pulaski, takes control of the Enterprise, and makes demands of his creators.

Given that this is episodic television, order is restored by the end of the hour and the computer program Moriarty "lives" to see another day. For Holmes aficionados, the episode offered a treasure trove of canonical references, including nods to "A Scandal in Bohemia," "The Speckled Band," and "The Red-Headed League."

A robust Moriarty returned to the decks of the Enterprise in the 1993 sequel episode, "Ship In A Bottle." A glitch in the Enterprise's computer causes Moriarty to reappear, and to wreak havoc among the Enterprise crew. We learn that during the time Moriarty has been a "saved" program he's been conscious of time passing, and has also acquired a girlfriend, the Countess Regina Bartholomew. Keeping the subsequent mind-twisting plotline in order was so difficult that the *ST:TNG* production staff resorted to drawing diagrams for themselves during breaks in the filming schedule, in order to keep track of the complexities of the story.

Regardless of the era and medium, both the Sherlock Holmes and the *Star Trek* worlds each feature an extended cast of recurring characters who add depth and provide cultural context to the adventures. In Sherlock Holmes we meet Mrs. Hudson, arguably the most patient and forgiving ~~housekeeper~~ landlady in the history of rental agreements. While in *ST:TOS* we can assume Federation ownership of the physical Enterprise, who would argue that the emotional owner of that gracious deep-space science vessel is anyone other than Montgomery Scott, the stalwart Scottish engineer who earns his daily bread keeping his captain from turning his beloved ship into mottled molecules of scrap?

Although both Sherlock Holmes and Captain Kirk plunge into their adventures with a singular confidence bordering on off-putting egotism, they both know that a key factor to their success is the extended web of savvy and skilled associates who take action when needed at the command of their leader. I'm referring of course to the Baker Street Irregulars and the crew of the SS Enterprise. Possibly not a pairing that would mesh well at a holiday party, but there's no arguing each group knows their stuff and are to be utterly relied upon in crunch-time.

Turning to the key pair of characters in each story, in both cases we have a wonderful yin/yang, a rationalist paired with a gregarious, more socially adept partner who at times performs the role of cultural interpreter or conduit. Sherlock Holmes and Spock, the two rationalists in both stories, make every effort to convince themselves and their companions that they are logic machines, with bodies that serve as little more than "transport." But a key to their unending fascination is that we know, even when they themselves don't or won't admit it, that's not quite true.

"I never played Spock as a man with no emotions," says Nimoy in a quote to Nicholas Meyer. "On the contrary, I always played him as a man of deep passions who was continually struggling to keep them in check." Compare that with this quote about the detective from *Sherlock*'s Steven Moffatt: "He's repressed his emotions, his passions, his desires, in order to make his brain work better—in itself, a very emotional decision, and it does suggest that he must be very emotional if he thinks emotions get in the way. I just think Sherlock Holmes must be bursting!"

These men's struggles with emotion versus logic are hindered by self-comparisons to a close family member who seems to have won the battle of brain over body. Spock wishes to emulate his Vulcan father, Sarek, and at one point attempts to permanently purge all emotion through the ritual of "kolinar." Of elder brother Mycroft, Sherlock says that he is "my superior in observation and deduction," while the Mycroft in *Sherlock* muses "Caring is not an advantage." On the maternal side of things, both Spock's mother, former teacher Amanda Grayson, and Sherlock's mother, former mathematician M L Holmes, are highly intelligent, strong-willed women who, it appears, both set aside their careers to dedicate themselves to raising their unique offspring.

Even physically Sherlock and Spock share similarities. In *A Study in Scarlet*, ACD described Holmes through the words of his biographer: "In height he was rather over six feet, and so excessively lean that he seemed to be considerably taller." Spock in particular, and Vulcans in general, are presented as ectomorphs with slender frames and long, delicate fingers. Neither of these men are 98-pound weaklings, however. Watson describes to his readers in "The Adventure of the Speckled Band" Holmes's amazing ability to straighten out a previously bent steel poker, and in later stories references Holmes's atypical strength, his singlestick and boxing prowess, and of course his expertise at baritsu. Vulcans by nature exceed humans in every aspect of physical endurance and have the added ability to enter into another being's thoughts in the technique of mind-melding. Although it's inferred that Spock is a lesser example of Vulcan capabilities because he is half-human, he's utterly superior to any human in physical conflict.

In comparison, Watson's and Kirk's physical appearance falls somewhere between the mesomorph and the endomorph. Shorter than their companions, they are strong men with above average stamina, but can veer to paunch if efforts aren't maintained.

Neither Holmes nor Spock pursue romantic entanglements; for both men pure reason and logic must hold sway. For purposes of this particular argument I'm considering only original ACD/Granada/*Sherlock*, and *ST:TOS*, and setting aside many well-known post-ACD adaptations, from the Gillette play to the Laurie King stories on the Holmes side, and the whole Spock-Uhura thing in the J.J. Abrams movies.

Despite popular misconception, Holmes never had a "thing" for Irene Adler or for anyone else. In "The Adventure of the Devil's Foot," he flat-out tells Watson "I have never loved." Spock's few escapades in *amour* occur when he's off-ship and external forces affect his mind. He accepts Leila Kalomi's romantic overtures in "This Side of Paradise" because he's ingested a mind-altering spore produced by the local flora. In "All Our Yesterdays," Zarabeth successfully woos Spock on the planet Sarpeidon only because Spock and McCoy have been thrown far back in time, to an epoch when Vulcans were barbaric and highly illogical. (Don't think about that one too deeply. Great excuse, Spock.)

Even on home turf both Sherlock and Spock have their female admirers. Unrequited admiration, of course. Both Christine Chapel and Molly Hooper work in the medical profession, and funnily enough both experience intense embarrassment when their gifts are literally (plomeek soup) or metaphorically (a Christmas present) flung back at them by the men they pine after. Thankfully, in both instances the men realize how badly they've behaved and give atypically emotional apologies.

And while we're on the topic of male-female relationships, how about our loverboy James "T for Tomcat" Kirk, whose bedroom exploits span the galaxy. Settling down doesn't seem in the cards for the good captain, whose marriage to Carol Marcus produced a son but no long-term monogamous commitment.

No less a playa, John H Watson declares himself a man for the ladies, with "an experience of women which extends over many nations and three separate continents," although honestly Kirk comes out the clear winner in this yardstick since his job covers a lot more territory. Still, the doctor also takes himself off the marriage market after he meets the lovely Mary Morstan, but he too returns to bachelor life after the first Mrs. Watson is no longer in the picture. How many more wives Dr. Watson eventually collects is a question beyond the scope of this article.

No comparison between the two narratives is complete without noting the exceptionally devoted, loving friendships that sit as the beating hearts of both stories. On the face of it, the immense success of each relationship seems unlikely, as the individuals involved are distinctly dissimilar. Each of the two pairs features an intellectual loner who, we are given to understand, has chosen to have few close relationships of any nature before the more gregarious partner enters his life. Watson and Kirk act as social conduits, and on occasion, cultural interpreters. They each "get" their friend in a way others cannot, or choose not to. In return, they are rewarded with exceptionally perceptive insights and perspectives on a wide range of topics, especially those grounded in the sciences, although we can make a pretty firm bet that Spock knows more than Sherlock about the solar system. Ours, and everyone else's.

However, and this can get easily overlooked in the glare of Spock's and Holmes's brilliance, both friendships blossom from characteristics that all four men share. They are men of action and agency. Fundamentally, they live decent and moral lives. None of them are high-functioning sociopaths; they all have consciences. They exhibit wide-ranging curiosity about their world and their place in it. Despite the Nigel Bruce interpretation, Watson is smarter than the average bear, and Kirk even more so. Most critically, they celebrate and respect the differences between each other as much, or more, than the similarities.

Whether roaming the galaxies or back alleys, Kirk & Spock, and Holmes & Watson, live for, and would die for, one another in the course of their quests. How much of our attraction to these sets of stories is a smidge of envy in seeing these men experience the best of both worlds: the freedom of endless adventure coupled with the companionship of a soulmate?

So there you have it … and not even all of "it" by a long shot, but perhaps enough to start you off on your own game of "spot the similarities" the next time you find yourself anywhere near these narratives. Quick! How are *Without A Clue* and *Galaxy Quest* alike?

Live long & prosper … it's elementary.

✗

Lynne Stephens discovered both the *Trek* and Holmes worlds in her youth and has been merrily bifangual ever since. She cherishes the memory of meeting Roddenberry during a set visit to *STII: Wrath of Khan*. Lynne lives in Virginia and is a member of the Watson's Tin Box scion society.

RECURRING CHARACTERS IN THE NERO WOLFE STORIES

by Robert Goldsborough

Among the many enjoyable aspects of being the approved con-tinuator of the Nero Wolfe mystery series is the opportunity I have to draw on the large number of continuing characters Rex Stout created in more than seventy stories over a forty-year span.

And characters they are, indeed. This varied group cannot be termed an ensemble company—after all, Nero Wolfe and Archie Goodwin are demonstrably the stars of the show. This then is a true supporting cast, more than a dozen players who appear in vary-ing frequencies throughout the corpus, some of them occasionally playing major roles.

Those new to the Wolfe stories may find the descriptions that follow helpful as background. Longtime readers may find them-selves reminded of characters they had forgotten about or particu-larly liked.

FRITZ BRENNER appears in nearly all of the Wolfe stories and with good reason. The Swiss-born Brenner is Wolfe's live-in chef, the creator of three-star meals that Wolfe and Goodwin consume twice daily. A tiny sample of the Brenner artistry includes: duck-ling in Flemish olive sauce; shad roe *aux fines herbes*; pork fillets braised in spiced wine; lamb kidneys *bourguigonne*; *cassoulet castelnaudary*; sweetbreads in *béchamel* sauce; and filets of beef in sauce *abano*.

Fritz understandably takes pride in his artistry and does not ap-preciate Nero Wolfe questioning his decisions. A point of conten-tion: Fritz prepared shad roe in casserole with onions and Wolfe said no to the onions in one book, *The Mother Hunt* (1963). They argued heatedly and Rex Stout did not tell us who won, but were I a betting man, I would place my money on Fritz.

Despite the occasional argument with Wolfe over food prepara-tion, Fritz is intensely loyal to his employer and he frets if the great detective does not have a client and money isn't coming in to support the hefty expenses of the brownstone, including the food bills, the beer bills (Wolfe orders beer by the case), the books Wolfe reads, often three-at-a-time and the cost of maintaining the 10,000 orchids Wolfe grows in the fourth-floor greenhouse. Speaking of the orchids …

THEODORE HORSTMANN has been Wolfe's full-time orchid nurse seemingly forever. He has lived in the brownstone off and on during the long-running series, sometimes staying with a sister in New Jersey. He appears in far fewer stories than Fritz and he rarely has a speaking part. Archie doesn't like him and the feeling is mutual.

Horstmann is fiercely protective of Wolfe and the orchids and whenever Archie has to bother Wolfe with business during his inviolate four hours a day (9-11 a.m. and 4-6 p.m.) upstairs with the orchids, Theodore is furious. For that matter, Wolfe is hardly happy himself when he is interrupted during his orchid hours. Rex Stout tells us very little about Horstmann and as a result, he is the least-interesting character in the cast.

LILY ROWAN has been Archie's "special friend" almost since the beginning of the corpus. In the sixth Wolfe book, *Some Buried Caesar*, Archie happens to be in a meadow in Upstate New York while working on a case with Wolfe and a bull charges him. He leaps over a fence to avoid the animal and sprawls on the ground, banging a knee.

"Beautiful. I wouldn't have missed that for anything," chirps a young woman in a yellow shirt and slacks who had been watching the drama. She ends up steering him to a telephone and he says, "I realized with surprise that her head came to my chin or above and she was blonde but not at all faded and her dark blue eyes were not quite open …"

This was Archie's introduction to Lily, who would be his very good friend for the rest of the series. Because of his pasture antics, she tagged him with the name "Escamillo" after the "toreador" in the opera "Carmen" and she continues to call him that. Lily is beautiful, rich and lazy. Her money comes from her late father, an Irish immigrant who made millions building New York City sewers. It also has been said of Lily's father than he got Cramer his job on the police force.

Lily lives in the penthouse of a building on Sixty-Third Street between Madison and Park Avenues that has a white grand piano and walls adorned with paintings by Renoir, Cezanne, and Monet. She also owns a summer place north of New York and a ranch in Montana. She throws parties at her penthouse that Archie attends, of course, and they frequently go dancing—Lily is the best dancer he knows—and attend Rangers hockey games at Madison Square Garden. Archie makes the point that despite Lily's wealth, when they go out on the town, he pays—period. As to the extent of their relationship, only they know the details and they're not talking.

SAUL PANZER is the best of the freelance operatives Wolfe uses and it is a rare case in which he does not make an appearance. Saul's own appearance is not impressive: He's 5 feet 7 inches, weighs in at 140 pounds, has a face that's about two-thirds nose and usually needs a shave. But do not let that appearance fool you. He is, as Archie says, "the best head and foot detective west of the Atlantic." Nobody can hold a tail better than Saul and he will drop anything else he's working on to give Wolfe a hand.

Wolfe for his part holds Saul Panzer in high esteem, having said he trusts him "further than might be thought credible." A bachelor, Saul lives in quarters on the top floor of a house on East Thirty-Eighth Street. His spacious living room has large bookcases, fine art on the walls, and a grand piano—which he plays. His abode is home to a weekly poker game in which he is usually the winner. Ask Archie.

FRED DURKIN is also a freelance operative regularly employed by Wolfe and Archie. While not is Saul's league, the thickly-built Fred, with a face like the map of Ireland, is fiercely loyal to Wolfe and according to Archie, he is "as honest as sunshine, but [not] so brilliant as sunshine." Wolfe once told a client that "Within his capacity, he is worthy of your trust and mine." Archie, impressed with Fred's skill at surveillance, once asked how he did it. "I just go up to the subject and ask him where he's headed to, and then if I lose him, I know where to look."

"I suppose he knew how funny he was," Archie said. "I don't know. I suspect him."

ORRIE CATHER, the third freelancer who most often appears in the Wolfe stories, is handsome and self-possessed to the point of arrogance. He has an eye for the ladies and thinks he could do the job of being Wolfe's right-hand man better than Archie. Wolfe has said of Orrie: "I have no affection for him; he has frequently vexed me; he has not the dignity of a man who has found his place and accepted it."

Suffice it to say, Orrie ultimately proves unworthy of Wolfe's trust.

BILL GORE, JOHNNY KEEMS, THEODOLINDA (DOL) BONNER and *SALLY CORBETT* are operatives used sparingly by Wolfe and Goodwin. Dol Bonner also appears as the protagonist in her own Stout mystery novel, *The Hand in the Glove* (1937).

DEL BASCOMB is a well-thought-of private investigator who runs a large Manhattan detective agency. Wolfe sometimes subcontracts to Bascomb when he needs additional men on a case. In once recommending him to someone seeking a detective, Wolfe referred to Bascomb as "a good man."

INSPECTOR L. T. CRAMER is head of homicide for the New York Police Department and Nero Wolfe's most frequent sparring partner. Although tough and well-regarded, the burly Cramer has a short fuse and his exasperation over Wolfe's involvement in murder cases frequently boils over and he often ends up storming out of the brownstone after throwing an unlit cigar at Wolfe's office wastebasket—and missing.

Cramer—in my stories I have given him the first name of Lionel because he *seems* like a Lionel—has had a complex relationship with Wolfe. For all of the *sturm und drang* in their relationship, they have a grudging respect for each other. Wolfe recognizes that Cramer is a fearless and honest cop and the inspector recognizes Wolfe's brilliance. At the end of each story when Wolfe reveals the culprit, Cramer is invariably present to make the arrest.

Cramer appears as the protagonist of one Rex Stout novel, *Red Threads* (1939), in which he capably solves a case that does not involve Nero Wolfe or Archie Goodwin.

SERGEANT PURLEY STEBBINS, Cramer's sidekick, is roundly disliked by both Wolfe and Goodwin. Purley is tall, broad and stocky—190 pounds—with a bony face, big ears and a square jaw. He has no sense of humor whatever and he is always upset in the presence of Wolfe and Archie, neither of whom he trusts. Says Archie: "Purley and I have often been enemies and even friends once or twice."

LIEUTENANT GEORGE ROWCLIFF is even more disliked than Stebbins in the old brownstone. He is handsome and has earned a medal for his police work, but he has pop-eyes and a tendency to stutter when he is upset, which is usually his state when in Archie's presence. "I would enjoy a murder where Rowcliff was the one who got it," Archie once said. To Wolfe, Rowcliff is "the officer who came here once with a warrant and searched my house."

COMMISSIONER HUMBERT, COMMISSIONER SKINNER and *DEPUTY COMMISSIONER O'HARA* are among the other members of the New York Police Department who make occasional appearances in the corpus. Wolfe calls Humbert "a disagreeable noise" and Skinner is referred to as "a slick rabble-rouser" by no less than the U.S. Secretary of State in one of the stories.

Non-New York City law enforcement figures who find their way into the stories are *WESTCHESTER COUNTY DISTRICT ATTORNEY CLEVELAND ARCHER, BEN DYKES*, a Westchester County detective, and *CON NOONAN*, a lieutenant in the New York State Police who dislikes Wolfe and Goodwin (see the novella *Door to Death*).

ASSISTANT DISTRICT ATTORNEY IRVING MANDELBAUM, who appears in several cases, is plump, short, balding and big-eared. But though he isn't impressive in appearance, he is businesslike and self-assured. Wolfe and Archie can abide him better than many of the other city officials they have occasion to cross paths with.

LON COHEN of the *New York Gazette* is a good friend of Wolfe and Archie and an occasional dinner guest in the brownstone. He does not seem to have a title at America's fifth-largest newspaper, but he has the ear of the paper's publisher and seems to know nearly everything that goes on in the city. Wolfe and Archie have tapped his knowledge many times on cases and Lon has been repaid with numerous scoops for the *Gazette*.

Lon is well-dressed and dark-complexioned, with dark eyes and slicked-down black hair. He is fond of highballs and good food, particularly steaks, and he is the second-best poker player Archie knows, after Saul Panzer.

DOCTOR EDWIN A. VOLLMER, who lives just down Thirty-Fifth Street from the brownstone, has performed a variety of services over the years for Wolfe, Archie and their clients. Vollmer is a little guy with a high forehead, a round face and not much chin. But he is dependable and discreet. He is one of the people Wolfe really likes and he is an occasional guest for dinner in the brownstone.

NATHANIEL PARKER is the only lawyer Nero Wolfe feels he can trust. Parker, who appears in several of the stories, is middle-aged, 6 feet 4, and lanky. He is one of the few people Wolfe shakes hands with and he also is one of the relatively few who occasionally dines in the brownstone.

LEWIS HEWITT is a wealthy man-about-town and patron of the arts with a sprawling estate at North Cove, Long Island. He also is an orchid fancier whose own collection rivals that of Nero Wolfe. He appears in several of the stories and he and Wolfe have done favors for each other. In one instance, he recommended someone as a client to Wolfe.

MARKO VUKCIC was Nero Wolfe's closest friend, going back to their boyhood years in Montenegro, and he was the only person who called Wolfe by his first name. Moving to New York, Marko opened Rusterman's Restaurant, which appears in numerous stories. Marko is shot dead in Manhattan and in search of his killer, Wolfe and Archie travel to Montenegro in *The Black Mountain* (1954).

After Marko's death, Wolfe was named trustee of Rusterman's and continued to eat there at least once a month. The restaurant, one of the finest in New York, appears in numerous stories.

HERB ARONSON (Archie's favorite) and *AL GOLLER* are New York cab drivers who appear in the series to perform surveillance and miscellaneous other duties.

ARNOLD ZECK is Nero Wolfe's *bête noire*, a true prince of darkness. This master criminal and Wolfe face off against each other in a trio of books, *And Be a Villain*, *The Second Confession* and *In the Best Families*. Later these three were consolidated in a Nero Wolfe Omnibus titled *Triple Zeck*.

This saga encompasses (1) a machine-gunning of the green house on the roof of Wolfe's brownstone, (2) Wolfe leaving home on an extended period and returning to New York many dozens of pounds lighter and (3) the permanent removal of Arnold Zeck. It ends with Archie and Lily Rowan vacationing among the fjords of Norway.

Wolfe's home, the old brownstone on West Thirty-Fifth Street, also appears as a regular "character" in the series. The four-story structure consists of: a first floor with Wolfe's office, the front room, the dining room and the kitchen; the second and third floors have bedrooms; and the fourth-floor houses the rooftop greenhouse that includes three climate-controlled rooms—cool, moderate and tropical—for Wolfe's ten thousand orchids.

And we must not forget the elevator, which measures four feet by six. Wolfe uses it several times daily for round trips to the greenhouse and for any other ventures that necessitate his moving between floors. There also is a second "lift" in the brownstone, in essence a dumbwaiter located in the backstairs hallway and running from the basement to the roof. It is used to carry trash as well as supplies for the orchids.

Throughout the corpus, ten different addresses on West Thirty-Fifth Street—from 506 to 938—are given for the address of the brownstone. The larger of these numbers would place the home of Nero Wolfe well into the Hudson River! But then Rex Stout was not always a stickler for details, which is one of the many reasons why the series is so interesting and so much fun to read.

✗

Robert Goldsborough is the author of fifteen murder mysteries, including ten featuring Nero Wolfe and Archie Goodwin. His eleventh Wolfe novel, *Stop the Presses!* was published in the spring of 2016.

SP

A TIGHT FIT

A NERO WOLFE ANECDOTE

by Marvin Kaye

It was going to be a busy day, but at the moment I had no idea just how busy it was about to become. Said moment was 3:45 in the afternoon. I was catching up on the orchid germination records while Wolfe at his desk read Cameron Rogers's biography of Savinien de Bergerac, who I gather was the real-life model for Edmond Rostand's theatrical swordsman Cyrano.

The office was nice and quiet, but it wouldn't remain so because by eight that night we would be visited by a roomful of guests, some of them doubtlessly irate, while one would be very worried, as well he (she?) might when Wolfe revealed the identity of the murderer. Which meant Inspector Cramer would be there, too, along with Sergeant Purley Stebbins.

I had a few things to do to get ready for Wolfe's charade, such as replenishing our stock of bottles, but I was going to wait till Wolfe went up to the plant rooms. Just then, his chair creaked and he rose. It was four o'clock and the orchids were waiting.

Outside, Manhattan was caught in the grip of a fierce snowstorm. The streets were impassable, and buses weren't running; people who lived any distance away were leaving work early while the subways and trains were still functioning.

Since I was at my desk, I didn't see Wolfe in the hallway step into his elevator, which was never easy for him since he came close to filling it. I heard him, though, muttering to himself about the tight fit, and I also heard the clang of the gate and the metallic protest as the elevator began its ascent …

And then all of the lights suddenly went out.

"Archie!" Wolfe bellowed.

"Coming." I groped my way into the hall. "What's wrong?"

"I'm stuck."

"Stuck? How?"

He growled. "In the elevator, dolt!"

I counted to five, and then said, "I don't answer to that."

He exhaled a bushel of air. "I'm sorry. Get me out of this thing."

"How?"

Another deep breath. "By restoring the electricity, of course."

"Okay. Hold on. I'll see what I can do." I fumbled back to the office, found a flashlight and switched on the radio. I learned that the city had just suffered a major power outage. I returned to Wolfe and told him about it.

After a silent moment, he said, "Very well, never mind the orchids. But I need to escape this cage—and soon! What can you do?"

"I've got an idea. Hopefully, we'll get lucky." I hurried to my desk and picked up the phone, which, mercifully, still worked. I aimed my flashlight at the Rolodex and found the number for Jimmy Donnelly, who supervised the elevator's original installation. He picked up and I told him our problem.

"I can fix that," he reassured me. "I'll have to bring a big battery, but I've got one to spare. I'll be over first thing in the morning, weather willing."

"No, Jimmy! It's got to be now. We've got people and police coming here tonight."

"But Archie, be reasonable! I can't tote that heavy battery through this mess."

"Not even," I improvised, "for a bottle of scotch?"

"Blended or single malt?"

"One of each," figuring Wolfe would not object to the expense.

He took a few seconds, then demurred. "It'll be too hard. I can't manage it."

More improv, and this time riskier. "Two bottles of scotch and a meal prepared by Fritz?"

No pause. "I'll be there!"

You may now thank me because during this conversation, I've spared you Wolfe's frequent importunate bellows.

I went to the hallway and reported.

"Satisfactory," he grunted. I thought he was done but after a short silence, he surprised me by saying—and I swear he sounded embarrassed—"There's something else you have to do for me."

"Yes? What?"

And he said something that I have never ever imagined would pass his lips!

"Archie, I drank too much beer."

I turned into a statue.

"Archie, did you hear me?"

"Yes. But what am I supposed to do about it?"

"Ask Fritz to give you a large empty bottle and bring it here."

"And then what?"

"Hold it for me."

My first impulse was to go outside and make a snowman, but decency restrained me. "Mr. W.," I said, "that is not in my job description."

"Archie, *please*!"

"All right. I'll get a jug." As I returned, I said, "This is going to cost you."

"How much?"

"Triple my salary."

"You know," Wolfe said, "I could aim for your head."

"Double my salary."

"Oh, very well."

"Wait till I write it and you can sign it."

"ARCHIE!!!"

I grinned. "Just kidding." I lofted the jug. "Here it is."

Let us mercifully pass over the ensuing event.

✗   ✗   ✗   ✗

Jimmy Donnelly arrived, red in the face and panting. The battery was enormous. I had to respect him; I had no idea he was this strong. He told me, "Archie, this going to take a while."

"How long?"

"No idea. But it'll be way more than an hour."

I led him to the hall so he could say hello to the elevator's prisoner.

The day slowly passed and it was evening. The engineer was still at it when Cramer and Purley arrived and soon after the guests began to appear, all of them grousing about the darkness, as if it were our fault.

Well, there was nothing we could do but bring them into the hall where Wolfe began to expound to them from on high, which, of course, he often does, but this time it was literal. He finally revealed the murderer's identity and Cramer took her into custody. Just then, the lights came on and the elevator brought Wolfe down to the hall. He got out and, ignoring everyone, including me, went into the kitchen for his long-delayed supper. (He later told me that Fritz outdid himself.)

✗   ✗   ✗   ✗

I was back in the office finishing the germination records when Wolfe poked his head in and told me that he was going to bed and should not be called for any reason till he came down tomorrow, which he might not do.

"But what if the house begins to burn?"

"Not even then!" And he turned away.

I was curious, so I got up and followed him to see what he would do. He then did something that I have never seen before.

He climbed the stairs.

✗   ✗   ✗   ✗

Wolfe was good as his word. My salary doubled for the rest of the year and throughout the winter. But when it finally got warmer, he told me, "I have paid quite long enough for one moment's relief, and I am no longer embarrassed by it."

And he cut me back to my old salary.

So for the sake of further embarrassment, I've decided to tell you all about it.

✗

Marvin Kaye is the author of seventeen novels and numerous short stories, as well as the editor of best-selling anthologies, *Sherlock Holmes Mystery Magazine*, and *Weird Tales* magazine. A native of Philadelphia, he is a graduate of Penn State, with an M.A. in theatre and English literature.

THE STRANGE DISAPPEARANCE OF MR. WELLS

by Ashley Lynch-Harris

Months ago, an unexpected reunion with my friend and private investigator, Hugo Flynn, resulted in our joint efforts to solve a rather curious case concerning one man and *both* of his deaths. He was a bit over ambitious if you ask me, but there it was—the case that started our partnership. Having been down on my luck at the time, and having nowhere else to go, I took residence in one of Hugo's extra rooms and in exchange I've assisted my friend in his various cases, documenting some of the more interesting crimes for my periodical, *The Sleuth's Observer*. The case which I am going to expand on now has already garnered much attention in newspaper headlines, but it is the lesser known case which started it all that has been of particular interest to my colleague and me. I refer, of course, to the *Lunford Museum Robbery*.

It was the third Tuesday of July, just after breakfast, when Hugo remarked on a nervy woman pacing about anxiously on the stoop of our apartment building.

"She is certainly indecisive," he mentioned casually, moving his hand from the drapes. "Will she ever enter the Promised Land, I wonder. She's come this far."

"Perhaps your growing fame intimidates her," I suggested.

Turning his back toward the window he shrugged, tossing a newspaper in my direction.

"We might as well pick a crime from the headlines. We haven't had a case in *weeks*."

As I considered our options, Hugo stretched his skinny frame across the couch, the lapels of his new blazer crumpling against his chest as he pressed a pillow onto his face in anguish.

"Come now," cooed Mrs. Hubbard, Hugo's irreplaceable live-in housekeeper. "It can't be as bad as all that, Huey dear," she consoled, her wrinkled hand pouring us a cup of tea. "I'm sure there will be a nice robbery—oh, or better yet, you never know when there might be a mean old serial killer on the loose," she added, squeezing his shoulder encouragingly.

"Yes, Mrs. H, one can only hope," I said dryly.

Turning the paper over, I asked my friend, "How about the man who was shot to death in South Kensington?"

Based on Hugo's muffled response I deduced he had little interest in that particular case.

"A robbery, perhaps?" I asked, turning the page. "Apparently some sort of jewelry box—almost a thousand years old—was stolen from the Lunford Archaeological Museum last night, and the archaeologists are in hysterics. Worth quite a lot of money, it seems. Someone swapped the genuine artifact with a fake one while it was in transit." I was pleased to find that this article seemed to elicit at least some interest from the detective. His face emerged from beneath the pillow.

"Any leads?" he asked.

"Authorities are looking into the two drivers who were commissioned to transport the artifact. One apparently has deposited large sums of money into his account within the last few months."

Hugo groaned and slipped back under his pillow. As terrible as it sounds, I was actually disappointed that the authorities had a viable lead, for Hugo's sake. At the sound of the doorbell, however, Flynn completely discarded my efforts and leapt forth from his sofa, his dress shoes sliding across the hardwood floor.

"Oh, *please* let it be a poisoning or maybe a political scandal— a shocking case of double homicide!"

I sighed, knowing that Hugo's thoughts were not limited to the company of friends alone. Is it any wonder, I considered, that clients are fearful to enter through our door! Fortunately, the nervous woman of whom we previously remarked had summoned the courage to do so.

From across the threshold I observed a rather homely-looking, middle-aged woman of average height, and I'm afraid (by way of first impression) Hugo's excitement for a scandalous affair faltered. Still, we were hopeful.

Her features were not remarkable by any means, with exception of her eyes. They were sharp and alert—clever, and I recall thinking very strongly to myself that masked behind that mundane veneer was, I expect, an incredibly intelligent woman.

"Please, have a seat, Ms …?"

"Mrs. Wells," she stated promptly, studying Hugo. "Julia … Wells,"

Gently placing the now-disheveled sofa pillow behind her, she discreetly divided her attention between the two of us.

"Oh, and this is David Merrick," introduced Hugo hastily. "A colleague of mine."

My eyes settled briefly upon Hugo as I waited for him to wave his hand in dismissal. Such a gesture, I felt, would have been fitting for such an unflattering introduction. My slight annoyance, however, was quickly extinguished as I attributed his behavior to sheer eagerness. I was proved correct when Hugo rushed to a seat across from Mrs. Wells and immediately seized his quarry.

"Now what seems to be the problem, Mrs. Wells?" he asked, salivating.

Hesitating, the client's eyelashes fluttered downward, her fingers pulled at a loose thread on her pants. Hugo, ever faithfully awkward in relating to others, "encouraged" our client.

"Death? Poisoning, perhaps?" he asked, hopeful. "Found a body, have we? Not sure what to do with it?"

The now-wide eyes of Mrs. Wells returned to meet the detective's. I fully expected Hugo's eyebrows to dart up and down in joyous anticipation.

"Please," I interjected. "Share with us why you've come. As you can see," I glanced toward Hugo reproachfully. His expression, in turn, was one of incomprehension. "We deal with all sorts of problems," I continued. "I'm sure what you've got to tell us won't be all that unfamiliar."

Studying me briefly, Mrs. Wells nodded. "All right," she began. "I suspect my husband of having an affair—"

Hugo's eager expression deflated considerably to say the least, so much in fact Mrs. Wells became mildly panicked, bursting forth in speech.

"No, you don't understand," she reassured him. "As I said, I suspect—or perhaps suspected my husband of having an affair …"

Mrs. Hubbard offered her a glass of water, which she accepted.

"The last few weeks he has been acting so strangely. Last night he told me he had to go somewhere for work. Not believing him, I followed him when he left the house. He pulled into a hotel."

Mrs. Wells's voice broke. Pausing, she took a sip of her water.

"Before you continue," I began, "in what way was your husband acting strangely?"

"Oh, I suppose 'strange' in the usual sense that one would expect if your spouse were hiding something. For instance, coming home later and talking to me less ... taking calls in a way so that I don't overhear him."

I nodded. "Please continue. What happened when you followed your husband?"

"As I said, I suspected my husband of having an affair so I discreetly followed him to the hotel room and watched as he entered. I crept closer and listened just outside the door. I heard his voice—he has a very distinct, raspy voice—much like someone's voice would sound if sore from yelling. Anyway, I knew he must have been talking to someone—his mistress, no doubt."

Mrs. Wells's hand shook as she took another sip of her water.

"I remember," she continued, "that when I was standing just outside the door he said, 'I've got it now. Let's go.' I waited until I heard another voice in the room. I couldn't make out the words, but I was sure there was someone in there with him. I saw the housekeeper walking down the hall (she must have just finished cleaning the room next door), and I threw a fit, telling her I locked my baby in the room, and I needed her to open the door immediately because I left the water running in the tub. That was the first thing that came to mind to get her to open the door without any questions."

Clever, I thought to myself.

"The maid didn't hesitate," explained Mrs. Wells. "We flung open the door, and I rushed in expecting to have my proof, and ..."

Mrs. Wells stared blankly past us, her forehead wrinkling in bewilderment.

"What happened, Mrs. Wells? What did you see?"

"Nothing," she stated softly, puzzled.

"Come now, Mrs. Wells," I encouraged. "You can tell us. You've said this much already."

Turning her blank gaze toward mine she repeated:

"Nothing …"

Blinking, she rubbed her head as if in pain. "Nothing *is* what I mean to tell you. There was nothing! No one was there! Not my husband, not a mistress, not even a pulled out chair or glass of water to tell me that someone had at least *been* there. My husband, you see, went into that hotel room and never came out."

Pinching the bridge of her nose, she added under her breath: "And I haven't seen him since."

"And this was just last night, you say?" asked Hugo.

Mrs. Wells nodded tiredly.

"Have you gone to the police?" I asked.

"I have," she said. "But since he hasn't been gone even a full day they say they can't treat it as a missing persons case."

Turning toward Flynn, she added, "But I was there, Mr. Flynn. I literally followed him into that room, and he never came out."

"Was there a balcony—windows?" asked Hugo.

"Yes, there were windows, but no balcony. It was a room on the first floor. The windows were blocked because of some construction next door—heavy machinery is blocking the entire first floor. You can only push the window open about a foot, if that much. And before you ask, no—there was not a connecting door to any other room."

"So you are suggesting your husband just vanished?"

"Well … *yes*. That's *exactly* what I'm suggesting!"

✗ ✗ ✗ ✗

Hugo and I arrived at the Sleeping Willows Hotel just after ten. Set in the historic district of Kensington, the quaint hotel was no more than three stories and still maintained much of its original architectural integrity. The owner and acting manager of the hotel, Mr. Charles Needling, was, in my opinion, an odd sort of man, in both appearance and manner. He reminded me very much of one of those hairless, wrinkled cats with a wisp of thinning hair at the top of its head. His shoulders had the habit of sinking forward when he walked and he seemed to perpetually hold the palm of his hands closely to his chest, anxiously moving them in circles around each other. He was, however, particularly helpful, offering us unlimited access to the room in question, and expressing great sympathy for Mrs. Wells, who accompanied us during our inquiries at the hotel.

"As you can see," explained Mr. Needling, sliding his guest book across the table toward us, "Mr. Henry Wells reserved this room exactly one week ago." Pushing his glasses further up the bridge of his nose, he added: "We reserved room 102 for Mr. Wells, and he even paid for the entire week in advance. Everything checked out from our end, you see? By the book—that's how I run my hotel."

"Did he specifically ask for Room 102?" asked Hugo.

The manager shook his head. "No, he just wanted a room on the first floor—he said something about the stairs being a hassle." Shrugging, the manager stood. "Would you like to see the room?"

We expressed that we would, and it was just as Mrs. Wells described.

"There's certainly only one way in or out," confirmed Hugo aloud while pressing the window open as far as possible. "It stops just short of a foot," he added, roughly measuring the gap with his forearm. Peering out the small space, he asked, "Just one other room to the left here until you reach the hotel's entryway, Mr. Needling?"

"Yes, yes," stuttered the owner excitedly, slicking back his dark, thinning hair with a shaky hand. "Facing the window you can see the window of room 101 to your left and, if the construction materials weren't in the way, you would be able to see the window to room 103 to your right." Turning the keys over in his hands, he added, "We have two entrances to the hotel. One from Haven Street, which you entered from, and the other from this side," he pointed toward Hugo. "That's Lunford Avenue. Not many people come or go from that side, however, because of all the construction. Blocks this entire side of the first floor," frowned Mr. Needling. "Not good for business. Not good for business at all," he mumbled.

"Who is staying in the room on the left?" asked Hugo.

A bit taken aback, Mr. Needling rapidly blinked. "Quite … quite. Room 101 … Yes! That's Mr. Jerry Lumpkin," he answered. "He's an older man visiting from Nebraska—or was it Nevada?" He frowned. Looking toward the detective, he added: "He's been here a little over a week now. The room is free if you would like to inspect it as well … although I'm not sure why that would help."

Mr. Needling frowned once more, his mind seeming to work tirelessly on the problem.

"Free?" I asked, bringing Mr. Needling back to the present. "Has Mr. Lumpkin gone?"

The hotel owner nodded. "Checked out this morning, as a matter of fact."

Static buzzed through Mr. Needling's radio as one of the maids called for his assistance.

"If you'll excuse me. Please let me know if there is anything you need. I will unlock Mr. Lumpkin's room on my way out … if you need to go in there." Turning toward Mrs. Wells, he added: "Again, Mrs. Wells, I am so very sorry for whatever has taken place." Rubbing his palms against his pants, he added, "It's an unusual situation, and I'm sorry it has happened at my hotel."

Turning away in haste, the manager lumbered hurriedly toward the doorway.

"Mrs. Wells?" asked Hugo. "You said a maid granted you access into this room. Would you locate her so that we might have a word?"

"Of course."

I watched as Mrs. Wells left the room before remarking to Hugo, "Why the interest in the adjacent room? Do you think Mr. Wells might have gone in there instead of this one? Perhaps Mrs. Wells was mistaken?"

"Possibly," replied Hugo. "But I'm more interested in its smell." Leaning on the desk that was situated just under the window, Hugo briefly studied the space. In deep thought, he pulled his curly hair away from his rather large forehead (a feature growing in popularity almost as much as his reputation as a great detective).

"Strong … *strong* scent of citrus," he uttered aloud. Quite suddenly he propelled himself from the desk and strode toward the other room of apparent interest. "I don't think there is much left to see here," he remarked. "Let's take a whiff of the other room, shall we?

I lingered behind Hugo, feeling completely useless. Just as the room before, I saw yet another ordinary room, *identical* to the last. I discreetly took a few meager sniffs. This room also smelled fairly clean … perhaps not *as* citrusy, but clean nevertheless. Leaning against the doorframe, I watched as Hugo pressed the window in the same manner as before, producing the same results—a one foot gap that a body could not squeeze in or out of. Then I watched in bewilderment as he walked through the room, his nose twitching wildly like an excitable guinea pig.

"Interesting, very interesting" he remarked, inhaling and exhaling deeply this time. "I think that—Oh!"

Turning, I followed Hugo's startled gaze toward a considerably robust woman with a mass of frizzy red hair, which was restrained only by her maid's cap bound tightly atop her head, an accomplishment, I suspect, achieved only by sheer determination. Her flushed face was one of sincere enthusiasm, and I staggered backward as the maid's eyes met mine and she suddenly charged at us as if we were spectators on safari who had just gotten between a mother elephant and its baby.

"Edna Blevins," she declared, swinging her arm toward us.

With one firm shake she took us aside to explain what it was we were to look for.

"A man," she stated.

"A man?" I asked.

"Why yes! A man with a raspy voice," she added. "I heard him loud and clear. 'I've got it now. Let's go.' he said." Leaning in, Mrs. Blevins whispered. "That poor misses behind me. To have a cheatin' man. My Ben would never cheat on me, and if he ever did—woe the day!"

Mrs. Blevins thrust her arms upward, allowing her body to fall backward into a chair. Fanning herself, she added, "That would be the day, I tell you." She narrowed one eye at us knowingly.

Hugo, startled by such a self-assured ... lively woman, remained momentarily speechless. I took the liberty of beginning my own line of inquiry.

"Mrs. Blevins—"

"Call me Ms Edna, hun. No need to be so formal."

"Right," I started again, clearing my throat. "Ms Edna, can you tell us exactly what happened last night, starting from the time that you made the acquaintance of Mrs. Wells, please?"

"Of course! Like I said, there was a man—with a raspy voice!"

"Yes," I muttered. "Perhaps start a little before that, please. For instance, where were you?"

"Right." Mrs. Blevins reflected briefly, tapping a fiery red fingernail against her cheek. "I just finished cleaning the room next door—that's room number 103. No sooner did I push my cart out into the hallway when Mrs. Wells came running frantically towards me! Yelling about her baby being locked in the room, and the bath water was running. Needless to say, I'm a mom myself, and no babies were going up to the good Lord before their time—not on my watch! So I ran to the room and was inserting my key when I heard a man speak."

"The one with the raspy voice," I said.

"Right," continued Mrs. Blevins passionately. "I didn't have time to think it strange that a man was in there when Mrs. Wells was asking for help to get in. All I thought of was the baby. I burst through the door, and made my way straight to the tub. No child! No running water!

"Needless to say, I confronted Mrs. Wells about it, and when she told me …" Mrs. Blevins lowered her voice once more. "… about that cheatin' husband of hers …"

Edna smiled encouragingly toward Mrs. Wells, and continued, "… well I just said to her I don't blame her one bit! Not one bit! She had personal business to handle, and amen to that!"

Hugo, having recovered from his initial shock, asked, "Have you been responsible for cleaning Mr. Wells's room during the duration of his stay?"

Mrs. Blevins shook her head. "I would normally, because I am in charge of this entire floor. I clean each room like clockwork. The only time I won't clean a room is if the guests request as much by putting a 'Do Not Disturb' sign on the handle, or if they ask me personally when they see me in the hall."

"So Mr. Wells had the 'Do Not Disturb' sign up all week?"

"*Sure* did, except for yesterday. He left a note. He asked that I air out his room because it didn't have a fresh scent. I'll tell you what I did with that note! I snatched it up from that handle, that's what I did! Of *course* it wouldn't have a *fresh* scent! What does he expect if he doesn't let me *clean* the room?!"

Mrs. Blevins swung her wide hips toward Mrs. Wells, grasping Mrs. Wells's hand in hers. "I'm sorry, Mrs. Wells," started the maid, shaking her head sadly. "I've been trying to hold my tongue, but that husband of yours isn't worth it. No common sense, that man … and a cheatin' man at that." Mrs. Blevins shook her head solemnly once more. "Let him go, miss." Edna patted the petite hand she held in her palm. "You've just got to let-him-go."

Hugo coughed. "Yes, well," he started again. "Did any of the other hotel guests make the request that you were not to clean their room?"

"Yes, Mrs. Whitaker in room 112," replied Mrs. Blevins, releasing her grasp on Mrs. Wells. "And Mr. Lumpkin from this room," she pointed her finger toward the door. "Number 101. Mrs. Whitaker," continued Edna, "put up a sign just one day this week, and Mr. Lumpkin asked me personally yesterday morning when I happened to run into him in the hallway. He said he had a research project spread out all over his room and didn't want his papers disrupted. Sweet old man, that Mr. Lumpkin. Some sort of scientist, that one—or maybe an archaeologist?" Edna nodded. "That was it. Archaeologist. I remember thinking 'old bones digging up old bones.'" She grunted. "Not very nice when I say it out loud, is it? But there it is, if you want honesty. Still, I did say he is a sweet old man, didn't I?"

"Yes, well …" I started, coaxing Mrs. Blevins's attention back toward the problem at hand. "Did you notice anything out of the ordinary when you were in the room of Mr. Wells, or even in the hallway during the time you were assisting Mrs. Wells?"

"Not a thing. I didn't see anyone in the hall when I was helping Mrs. Wells because I was in the room the whole time. As far as when I was cleaning his room, there wasn't anything strange there either. I opened the window like he asked, did a quick cleaning—using my *lemon-scented* products—I save those for the fussy guests, and I left." Mrs. Blevins perched her head to the side thoughtfully. "*Although*," she added slowly. "I thought one thing was odd … his bed. I didn't have to make it. I thought to myself, this man has been here an entire week, *denying* my services, and he never slept in his bed? Then I thought perhaps he made it himself, but I doubt that. That bed was made expertly—like how I would have made it." She sniffed. "Like I said, he doesn't strike me as very bright." Mrs. Blevins glanced apologetically toward Mrs. Wells.

"And besides," she added. "Makes me wonder what he has had this room for if not for sleeping or reading the good Word. Doesn't want anyone to see him, whatever it is. Sinnin' no doubt. Drugs would be my guess. My mother always said—"

"Yes, quite," I interjected. "Thank you very much, Mrs. Blev— excuse me, Ms Edna. You have been more than helpful. Any other questions, Hugo?" I asked over my shoulder.

Hugo expressed that he had none. Mrs. Blevins marched out of the room, passing Mr. Needling on her way out.

"Any headway?" asked the hotel owner, peering over the rim of his glasses, settled comfortably on the tip of his nose.

"Not much," I replied in earnest, feeling even more disappointed with our lack of progress as I caught glimpse of Mrs. Wells's fallen expression.

"May I use your telephone, Mr. Needling? asked Mrs. Wells.

"Of course, Julia," he replied. "My office is to the left once you enter the lobby."

With a nod, Mrs. Wells excused herself, but I couldn't help but feel my discouraging remark provoked her sudden retreat.

"We've really got to make some sort of progress, Hugo. I feel terrible. This woman's husband is gone, and we've got nothing to tell her. I suppose we need to track down Mr. Lumpkin. He is the next closest witness to the case …"

Hugo smiled. "On the contrary, David, I already know exactly where Mr. Wells is."

Turning toward the hotel's owner, Mr. Needling, Hugo remarked, "David, meet our 'Mr. Wells.' Mr. Needling, you and your wife are under arrest."

✗   ✗   ✗   ✗

Awaiting the police's arrival, I successfully detained both Mrs. Julia Needling (formerly known as Mrs. Julia Wells) and Mr. Charles Needling in the original hotel room that had claimed so much of our attention. Although I was annoyed that Mrs. Needling drew us into some odd farce concerning her husband's disappearance, in fairness I couldn't help but ask Hugo what exactly they did wrong to warrant their arrest. Hugo explained:

"The search for 'Mr. Wells' actually had nothing to do with his disappearance," replied Hugo. "This whole farce of a case was simply a smoke screen to mask the real crime, which was the theft of the valuable artifact recently discovered by archaeologists. Mr. Needling himself, not expecting us to make the connection, remarked on all the construction just outside on *Lunford* Avenue. Recall, David, the headline you read earlier mentioning the jewelry box that was stolen from the Lunford Museum. It is only logical that the Lunford Museum would be located on Lunford Avenue. Now let me explain how it was done."

Mr. Charles Needling shifted uncomfortably in his seat.

"Edna, the maid, takes great pride in her work, and as such, she cleans each room (unless otherwise asked) with a systematic diligence. In her own words, she operates like 'clockwork.' As such, Mr. Needling and his wife know exactly when to expect Edna to finish cleaning room 103 as well as when she will proceed toward cleaning the supposed room of 'Mr. Wells' in room 102. Remember, it was only that morning that 'Mr. Wells' requested the window be left open to air. Edna makes her way down the hall and runs into the supposed Mrs. Wells (who is really Mrs. Julia Needling). 'Mrs. Wells' convinces Edna to unlock the room with her phony story of the child in danger, but only after she is certain Edna also heard the raspy voice of her husband, Mr. Wells, inside. The pair burst through the door, and Edna stampedes into the bathroom to rescue the infant she expected to be there, and there is no doubt in my mind that Edna, being such a spirited woman, rushed toward the bathroom without even a glimpse of the rest of the room."

I nodded strongly in agreement.

Hugo continued. "Mrs. Wells, however, does not go toward the bathroom. She heads straight to the open window that sits just above a writing desk. Recall, the window only opens far enough to fit something a foot wide or less. Taking advantage of this, Mr. Wells (who is really Mr. Charles Needling dressed in a disguise that is completely opposite in appearance to how he really looks) is standing on Lunsford Avenue at the same time that his wife is employing their charade with the maid. At the appropriate time, Mr. Needling slipped a recorder through the window and onto the desk, thus creating the voice Edna heard just before storming in. Mrs. Wells collects the recorder, hiding it in her purse, and meets Edna in the bathroom to explain the real reason she had her enter the room—to catch her cheating husband. Edna, ever sympathetic to the cause, spends time counseling Mrs. Wells, no doubt, and inadvertently remains in the room, out of sight of what's going on in the hallway."

"So, I'm assuming," I conjectured, "that while Mrs. Wells is talking to Edna, Mr. Wells is swapping the fake jewelry box with the security guard who was recently paid large sums of money. Just as the newspapers reported."

"Exactly," agreed Hugo. "Making sure, of course, to use the distinctly raspy voice of Mr. Wells while he speaks with the guard. This ensures that when the security guard, once caught, talks to the police, he will describe the man the Needlings want him to describe. Mr. Wells, with a raspy voice, who occupied room 102, has since vanished. Even an independent investigation was done by his wife to try and find him!"

"But then why," I asked, "did they have to keep Edna out of the hallway? After receiving the real jewelry box from the security guard, all Mr. Needling would have to do is get away, right?"

Hugo shook his head. "Not if they are going to use the disappearance of Mr. Wells from the hotel as their scapegoat. Most likely there will be witnesses or perhaps even security cameras outside the hotel. The couple counted on that. Mr. Wells, in disguise, makes the switch with the security guard and walks back into the hotel. Here is where this ruse of the vanishing husband becomes essential. Mr. Wells, with the stolen jewelry box, comes into the hotel and proceeds down the first floor hallway. Instead of entering room 102, in which Edna and Mrs. Wells are located, he enters Mr. Lumpkin's room 101. He can't have anyone see him enter that room, especially the opinionated Edna, because once the jewelry box is stolen they need everything to link back to Mr. Wells, with the raspy voice, who disappeared from room 102."

"So Mr. Lumpkin never really existed either!"

Hugo smiled. "No, it's rather easy to play an old man, isn't it, Mr. Needling? A white beard that covers the face, a cane, and perhaps a slow, careful walk around the hotel to convince the other guests and employees that old Mr. Lumpkin, dry as bones, is staying in room 101. Furthermore, Mr. Needling, you make sure you personally request Edna to leave your room until the next day so she has no chance of discovering your disguise or the stolen jewelry box. The following morning you check out as the kindly old man who has nothing to do with the robbery that will have been discovered that very morning. Once our failed investigation had concluded (you hoped), you and your wife would redirect authorities to the mysterious Mr. Wells. It was really all the wife's idea, of course," added Hugo, looking curiously at the odd, cat-like husband who sat anxiously in the corner.

I must admit, I was completely dumbfounded by Hugo's connection between the two crimes. To Hugo, however, it was only logical. Having sorted all the information, and most importantly, not discounting the seemingly unimportant information of the robbery he heard of earlier, he was able to find the true motive. Mr. Needling told us himself that his hotel business was struggling, and just across the street was a valuable artifact worth a great deal of money!

"It was really the familiarity in which your husband said your name, Mrs. Needling," added Hugo, "that gave me the final connection I needed. When you asked to use the phone, Mr. Needling called you by your first name, and with a familiarity that was natural. I thought, what if these two actually know each other, and once I started on that line of thought, the pieces fell swiftly into place!"

Mr. Needling apologized to his wife, and she consoled him with a reassuring strength. "We endeavored to do what we needed to, dear, and you and I won't apologize for that."

In a way, I found her constitution admirable (if only it had it not been misguided in its ideals). Turning toward Mrs. Needling, I asked, "Why in the world did you come to us for help? If you hadn't, you probably would have gotten away with it!"

"For credibility," she replied. "I needed to show the police that I had done all I could to find my husband, to make them believe that Mr. Wells was real … a man with a family—people who knew him, and also that Mrs. Wells was not a viable suspect. Once they started on my 'husband's' scent, I would remove this mundane attire, Mrs. Wells would disappear, and I would return to being my true husband's wife."

Mrs. Wells rose, removing the brown wig and shrugging herself free from the faded overcoat that engulfed her. It was here that I saw the full embodiment of the woman who truly lived behind the intelligent eyes of which I earlier remarked. Turning toward Hugo, she added, "I had no idea, Mr. Flynn, that you would be this good."

Hugo, in his true form, stammered an incoherent, embarrassed thank you, all the while struggling with where to put his arms: crossing them, uncrossing them, tugging at his blazer, sliding them inside his pockets, and then finally clasping them behind his back as he shifted his stance with his typical gracelessness.

"I think the police have arrived," I remarked, standing. Turning to Hugo, I smiled, adding, "If you will excuse me, *The Sleuth's Observer* has a breaking news report to run."

✗

Ashley Lynch-Harris is the author of *The Hotel Westend*, a novel *Publishers Weekly* has described as "a charming homage to the classic mystery…" She is an honors graduate of the University of South Florida and lives in Tampa with her husband, Alex. For more information, please visit www.AshleyLynchHarris.com.

GUESSING GAME

by Nick Andreychuk

"**D**o you have any idea why we're here?" Detective Chad Parsons asked his partner, Eric Kasey, who sat slumped next to him in the front seat of their unmarked police car.

Eric raised an eyebrow at him. "*You're* asking *me*? This was your lead, remember?"

"Yeah, I know. It's just that a tip-off from a pizza delivery guy who got paid with a hundred-dollar bill stolen from our lockup isn't much to go on. But don't mind me, I'm just bored."

Working undercover on a stakeout, the police officers were parked across from a ramshackle two-story house that looked to be well over a hundred years old. The various layers of peeling paint gave the house's exterior the mottled look of a tortoise shell. A rusted sedan of indeterminate domestic make sat in the driveway. No one entered or exited the premises in the past five hours.

To pass the time on stakeouts, the police officers regularly resorted to simple games like "I Spy," "Twenty Questions," and "The License Plate Game." They often made up their own games, as well.

"The guy we're after is a cop killer, so he's likely killed before," Eric said. "Let's make a guessing game of it."

"That's a morbid game, even for us," Chad said, "but I'll give it a shot."

Eric pulled out his notepad and wrote something down. "Okay, I've got a place in mind. Where do you think the body is?"

"How about the trunk of the car?"

"You'll have to be a little more imaginative than that."

"This old house probably has a dirt basement—it'd be easy to bury a body down there."

Eric smiled. "You're certainly right. I'm sure if we dug it up, we'd find lots of bodies. But this body's not buried."

Chad glanced up at the dirty attic window. "Some people hide everything away in their attics."

"You're not even close."

Chad looked up even higher to the chimney. "Well, what about the fireplace?" he asked. "It could have some loose bricks, and—"

"No."

"Okay," Chad said, "I've got it now: inside the walls!" Eric shook his head, so Chad tried again. "The freezer?"

"Good guess, but as the game goes, you're getting 'colder' ..."

Chad didn't like to lose, but he was stumped. "Okay, I give up. Where else could a dead body be?"

"Let's go look," Eric said. He got out of the car and strode over to the house.

Chad jogged after him and grabbed his partner's arm just before they reached the front door. "What are you doing? You're going to blow our cover!"

"Relax. We haven't seen any sign of life around here all day. Don't you want to see if the guy who ordered the pizza left any clues in here?"

Chad shrugged and released his partner's arm. Eric picked the lock and they entered the house. The place was empty—no furniture, no empty pizza boxes, nothing.

After they'd searched the rest of the house, they wound up in the kitchen and Chad pointed at an old dumbwaiter. "Aha! It has to be Colonel Mustard with the candlestick in the kitchen."

"Funny, but no," Eric said. "Besides, stuffing bodies in dumbwaiters has become clichéd."

Chad sighed. "Okay, I really do give up now. Where's the dead body?"

Eric shot him through the heart. "Right here."

✗

Nick Andreychuk is the Derringer Award-winning author of *Extinct* and *Singapore Sling*. His stories have appeared in numerous magazines and anthologies, such as *Hardboiled: Crime Scene*, *Suspense Magazine*, and *Woman's World*. His work has been collected in *Crime Dealers* and *Three Hits of Jack*.

DREAM A LITTLE DREAM OF ME

by Jeff Baker

Someone died at the shelter last night. I was there by accident. I was living there at the time. My last two jobs had gone belly-up within about a month-and-a-half of each other, and my unemployment ran out and I went through my savings (that last took about another month) and sold a bunch of my stuff. That let me keep my apartment for about another month but I was living on chips. When I finally lost the apartment I had nothing to my name but my clothes, my jacket, and two bags of Ruffles, and it didn't take me long to go through the Ruffles. Luckily I found out about the shelter when I was at the downtown library. The guy who died was sleeping right next to me; I didn't even speak to him before lights out.

They wake you up bright and early in the morning at these places to feed you breakfast, then they run you out of there for the day and you fend pretty much for yourself. They let you back in the evening, if you've reserved your spot to sleep at the shelter for a week. Floor mats courtesy of some rich donor, dinner courtesy of whatever charitable organization was feeling charitable. I was on my own for lunch. I had a few bucks the first week or so, not enough to pay any rent anywhere but enough to grab some lunch. With the gloomy mood I was in I didn't bother with anything other than a cheap bag of chips, which I'd finish off while walking around. The only good news was the state of California issued me a food card I could buy lunch with. This let me wander around town with something in my stomach at least.

The dead man had shown up a couple of days before, when we'd both arrived at the shelter to line up and get our weekly spot to crash out. ("No sitting down in line.") The only thing I noticed was that his shoes looked a lot better than mine. The only clothes I had were the jeans and shirt and jacket I was wearing and they had been a little worn looking before I'd spent the last few months sleeping in them. This guy's clothes certainly didn't look new, but they didn't look slept in either.

And I wasn't checking out his wardrobe, I was checking around to see how dangerous the other guys in line were. That day I spotted one wearing what looked like a genuine motorcycle jacket, one in fatigues, a bunch wearing a layer of shirts under old coats and a couple of youngish guys warily looking around wearing the telltale thin white shoes they issue to someone who just got out of prison. They usually didn't bother me. Looking at some of the nasty, brutish faces I was sharing sleeping quarters with, that bothered me. So, I usually spent my time at the shelter trying not to look like I was paying attention to anybody. The usual big city who-you-lookin'-at-not-me bit. Fortunately they had a TV on; usually they either played one of the news stations or a movie on DVD so I had something else to pretend to look at. Not listening was no problem; the volume was usually turned up full-blast. It was an education, just in case there were any swear words I'd somehow missed out on learning. I wasn't going to gripe too loudly. Most of these guys could have beaten me to a pulp and in the mood I was in I wasn't likely to care. I'd resigned myself to the fact that for now the shelter was home or at least a place to crash at night and to get fed a couple of meals a day. Not quite the fabled "three hots and a cot," but it had to do.

Sleeping at the shelter could be done if you took precautions. I slept in my clothes and made sure I had my wallet under my pillow. My "pillow" being my wadded-up jacket. I'd noticed a few people carrying their own dingy pillows. I hated the idea that anybody would be so used to this that they would get a pillow to bring to a shelter with them. I dozed off listening to the grumbling, farting, and snoring from my roommates, trying to be grateful for whatever celebrity who had donated the money for the floor mats we were all sleeping on. One of the last things I noticed was the guy in the shiny shoes was lying in the spot next to me. I dozed off thinking that I hoped things were better for the kids and their mothers who stayed on the second floor.

I remembered dreaming, dreaming something about a voice looking for something to read. Then I was awake, staring at the darkened room, remembering where I was for a moment, and then I heard the voice again.

"Reid … can't find … knows you, not me …"

It was the guy with the shiny shoes. He'd rolled over and was talking in his sleep as he tossed and turned. I reached my hand under my jacket-pillow and felt for my wallet. Still there. I breathed a little easier. The shoe man murmured something else and rolled over again, facing the other way. I lay there hearing the breathing of the others and a rippling gurgle from my stomach. I wondered what time it was and thought of my watch. Then I was out like a light. The next thing I knew there was dim light coming in through the window over the door. I could still hear the quiet breathing around me. I lay there for a moment, wondering if I could get back to sleep. I readjusted myself on the floor mat and rolled over on one side.

The man in the shiny shoes was laying there facing me. His eyes were wide open and his mouth was open, the whole thing giving him a look of complete surprise. I was the one who was surprised. He wasn't breathing. I hadn't seen a lot of dead people but he was definitely one of them. I reached over and prodded him gently with an outstretched finger. There was a crinkling noise. I tugged on his shirt, I didn't know why. I told myself it was to make sure he's dead. A hundred dollar bill dropped out of his shirt. I heard it fall to the floor, I looked around. No one else was awake. I pulled up more of his shirt. Money was pressed up between shirt and body, from what I could see it was lots of money. And all in hundreds.

I poked him with my finger again, and thought about putting my ear to his chest to see if I could hear a heartbeat. I also thought about the money. How much was there? Maybe a hundred thousand dollars at least. I imagined it in stacks on the table in my old apartment on Powell Street, imagined my counting it, buying a car and house with it. Better yet, buying lunch with it, someplace where I could sit down to eat and just kick back and relax afterwards. But the money wasn't mine and I wasn't a thief and I wasn't going to start stealing now. Besides, there was no way I would have been able to get away with taking it out of the building, and someone would have woken up and found me crouched over a corpse rifling through his clothes, taking money.

I lay back down and stared at the ceiling. What was he doing here when he had all that money?

"Say, man, what's with the dude?" came a voice from behind me. "He looks like a stiff!"

I glanced behind me. One of the older guys wearing a grubby raincoat and torn jeans with sweatpants underneath had propped himself up on an elbow and was staring at the dead man.

"I think he's dead," I said. "He woke up that way, I mean; I woke up and found him that way."

"Man, they better get him outta here so somebody else can have that space," the guy behind me said. "I'm goin' to the bathroom."

He stood up and stepped over the guy sleeping next to him. One of the guys spoke up without opening his eyes.

"Be quiet. It's early."

"Shhhh!" somebody else said. The man wandered off toward the bathroom. For all practical purposes I was alone with a corpse. I reflexively felt under my wadded-up jacket for my wallet and then stuffed it in my back pocket. I stared back at the dead man's face. Then I remembered where else I'd seen him, days before.

The Main City Library was right across the street from City Hall, and to my mind was a lot more help. The good thing about the library was they had air-conditioning and they let you sit down if you at least made an effort to read a book or a magazine. I usually busied myself on the computer, which they would let you use for an hour if you had a library card, one of the few things I still had. I would kill an hour zipping between meaningless websites and videos, thankful that I could immerse myself in that at least. A few days before I first saw the dead man I saw him in the second floor of the library, at one of the tables reading one of a stack of magazines. What I noticed about him first were the clothes. Neat, not too fancy but still stylish, crisp shirt, a very light blue, nothing garish. Matching tie, creased pants and well-shined shoes. I didn't notice clothes, especially other people's, until I started sleeping in the same clothes every night, like a character on Gilligan's Island. I wouldn't have given him a second glance except I really didn't have much else to do. Besides, he stuck out. He was a little over-dressed for the library. I walked past his table, close enough to see that the magazines the man was reading were all about economics and world finance. He didn't look up; he just glared down at the pages. I didn't get a look at his socks, I wasn't that obsessive.

I checked in at the desk, got a computer and spent the next hour staring at the screen, clicking from one site to the next. After my hour was up, I wandered around the main floor of the library, leafed through a magazine or two and generally pretended I had somewhere else to go.

I saw the man one more time, right before I left late that afternoon; he was on the computer with an increasingly frustrated look on his face. I didn't give him a second glance.

I turned away from the dead man on the floor. I nudged the guy sleeping on the other side of me. He sat up, blinking in the early-morning light.

"You got a cell phone?" I asked. (Not a stupid question, a lot of the guys I'd seen at the shelter carried cell phones.) "This guy's dead. Somebody needs to get an ambulance or call the cops or something."

The guy stopped blinking and leaned over and stared at the guy.

"I don't think he died by accident," I said.

The man who was leaning over screamed, right in my ear. He jumped to his feet and screamed again. By this time, everybody was awake and either talking or yelling. "Shut up," seemed to be a favorite. Somebody ran out of the room hollering for somebody in charge. And I was suddenly remembering what the dead man had said in his sleep: About Reading or someone named Reid, and "Can't find. Knows you not me." He had repeated it several times, I knew that.

I glanced around at the guys. I was thinking about the money, the money under the dead guy's shirt, and I started to realize why he was there. I stared at the crowd milling around in the room, stared at them from my position sitting there on the floor.

"Listen up, everybody, I don't want anybody leaving this room until we get this, well, investigated, you know." That was from the kid with the crew cut who manned the front desk in the mornings. He was standing in the doorway. He looked a little clueless but was big enough that, although there was some grumbling everybody was going to stay put. The men's room was at one end of the room on the wall opposite the main door. The emergency door had an alarm on it. Nobody was leaving right away, that was for sure. One of the older men who worked there walked over to the dead man and examined him. He stood up and shook his head.

"Dead. Smothered. And apparently loaded." He held up a handful of hundred-dollar bills. There was an appreciative wolf whistle from someone in the crowd. "Somebody call the police?"

The guy in the doorway nodded.

I looked around again and it hit me. I knew what had happened.

"We gonna have breakfast?" somebody asked.

"In a bit," the guy at the front of the room said.

It must have been about ten more minutes before a couple of uniformed officers walked into the room. One of them walked over to the body while the other started questioning the man in the doorway. That was when I got the other shelter worker to one side and told him what I'd figured out.

"Just ask him that one question," I said.

He stared at me for a moment and then made his way around the room until he was in front of a group of men, one of them wearing layered shirts under a couple of coats.

The shelter guy smiled pleasantly. "Your name's Reid, right?"

The man in the coats lunged for the door.

"Grab him!" the shelter guy yelled as he jumped after him. Crew cut guy tackled him as the cop he was talking to grabbed for the man's waist. They made a neat pile there in the doorway.

In the middle of all the commotion that followed, some guy kept asking if we were going to get breakfast now.

Between the cops and me, we were able to piece together what happened. The dead man's name was Wilson. He had ripped off the money from the company he worked for when he found that it was going to go bust. The cash had been in the safe, and the man's partner and Reid, who worked for an out-of-town branch, were simply going to rip off the money and leave the country. Wilson had arranged with a friend of his to lay low and be picked up and they would split the money. Wilson knew about Reid but had never seen him. That had been what he'd been talking in his sleep about. Reid had found out where Wilson was and had waited for his opportunity to either get the money or kill Wilson or both. Reid found out somehow that Wilson had decided to hide in the shelter where nobody would think to look for him.

"I'd guess Wilson's buddy tipped Reid off," one of the cops said. I nodded.

"It's my guess that Reid made his move this morning when everyone was asleep."

"How did you know Reid?" the cop asked me.

"The shoes," I said. "Reid was dressed in layers of clothes that looked like he'd been sleeping on the street, but his shoes looked like they'd been shined yesterday. The same as Wilson's. And I remember him carrying a pillow. Somehow that stuck out to me. But when I saw him this morning, the pillow was gone."

"You've got a good eye," one of the cops said.

I shrugged. "I don't have anything else to do."

They found the pillow Reid had smothered Wilson with, stuffed in the trash in the men's room. I spent a lot of the day at the police station telling the story. Then I went back to the shelter. I didn't hear whether they found Wilson's buddy yet.

The next afternoon I wandered into the library like I'd been doing the last few months. This time I bypassed the magazines and the computers and sat down at a table with the want ads and a notepad. I figured better late than never. And after the last couple of days, I knew where there's life there's hope.

✗

A regular columnist at Queer SciFi.com, Jeff Baker has been a stand-up comic and a deliveryman, among other things. His story "Hit One Out of the Park" appeared in *Sherlock Holmes Mystery Magazine* #8. His Facebook page is at "Jeff Baker, Author."

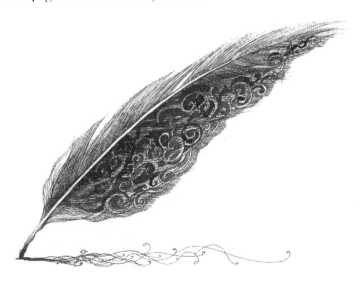

BURNED RIGHT DOWN TO THE GROUND

by Laird Long

Josh Evans was just unpacking his briefcase at his desk when Glenda Fellows walked into his office.

"There was another fire down in the Point Clair area last night, Josh," the claims manager said. "And this one might cost the company a lot of money."

There had been a string of arsons in the Point Clair inner-city neighbourhood during the past two weeks, everything from dumpsters to sheds to garages getting torched. A firebug (or bugs) at work.

"Hank's Hardware at the corner of Second Avenue and Elm Street," Glenda went on, looking down at the open file in her hands. "Burnt right down to the foundation, apparently. The owner, Hank Costic, phoned it in early this morning. He has a property policy with us for $500,000."

She closed the file and handed it to Josh. "It's your case now."

The claims adjuster nodded, restocking his briefcase.

He was at the smoldering scene of the fire fifteen minutes later.

There was little left of Hank's Hardware store but a sunken pile of scorched timbers and equipment, the only thing still standing the concrete foundation walls which rose up a couple of feet out of the ground all around. If this was the work of the firebug, he or she was getting better with practice.

"Mr. Costic?" Josh said, walking up to the forlorn-looking man standing on the sidewalk, staring at the mess. "I'm with Hilltop Insurance."

Costic didn't turn his eyes away from the business remains, his mouth open and lips trembling. His hand hung limp in the claims adjuster's hand.

Josh tried the policeman standing nearby. "Any witnesses, officer?"

He was more responsive, though no more helpful. "None," he said, shaking his head. "All the other stores along Second were closed and none of the people in the neighbouring houses on Elm saw anybody lurking around or setting a fire."

The officer glanced at the store-owner. "It looks like somebody broke in through a basement window and started the blaze from down there."

"That would explain the extensive damage, all right," Josh commented.

The three men walked along the sidewalk on Second Avenue, swung right onto the Elm Street sidewalk and then turned right again onto the small gravel parking lot at the rear of the fire-gutted store. The policeman pointed at the broken window in the foundation at ground-level.

"No footprints, unfortunately. Or fingerprints."

Josh squatted down and stuck his hand through the small opening.

"Careful!" the officer warned. "There's still some glass in the window frame."

There were a few jagged shards of smoked glass still sticking out of the blackened frame of the basement window. Josh withdrew his hand and pushed at the bottom of the window frame.

"There—there's a latch on the inside." Hank Costic spoke for the first time, pointing down at the window. His dull eyes were still fixated on the charred remains of the rest of the building.

Josh carefully put his hand back through the window and felt along the inside bottom of the frame. He found the latch and unhooked it.

"So there is," he said. "Thanks."

"The Fire Commissioner will be here around ten," the policeman stated, as Josh stood up again.

"My business—my life's work ... gone," Costic mouthed.

"Lucky you had insurance, sir," the policeman said, smiling at Josh.

"Yes," Josh said. "Only, it doesn't pay off, Mr. Costic, when you deliberately set fire to your own property and try to blame it on the neighbourhood arsonist."

Costic swung his head around and gaped at the claims adjuster. "What do you mean by that!?" He appeared even more stunned.

Josh explained. "If an 'outside' arsonist had broken into your store through the basement window, Mr. Costic, then either all of the glass would've been cleared out of the window frame so that he or she could get cleanly inside, or the window would've been unlatched. But since you have keys to the building and broke the basement window after you'd already set fire to your store, you obviously forgot about all that in all of the excitement."

The policeman clamped his hand onto Costic's arm, the store owner's fraud attempt up in flames.

⤴

Laird Long: Big guy, sense of humor; pounds out fiction in all genres. Has appeared in many anthologies and mystery magazines and resides in Winnipeg, Canada.

A PROCESS OF ELIMINATION

by Rekha Ambardar

Fay first noticed it two weeks ago—the excuses, the polite, but cool "how are you?" The appearance of being busy. Alan had cooled off. She tried to concentrate on the MSDS (Materials Safety Data Sheet), making sure that the updates were correct. From where she sat, she saw him talking to Nick, her assistant.

"I just want to make sure the piping on the air compressor is in working order—no breaks."

"Sure, go ahead, Dr. Kohner," Nick replied.

Fay glanced surreptitiously at Alan, who, although he knew she was there, placidly continued with his inspection of the Unit Operations Lab. He had on his safety glasses with the familiar red dot to indicate that he wore contact lenses.

She smiled sardonically to herself as she remembered that he hadn't wanted to let on that he wore contacts—vanity, perhaps? But why bother? As far as looks went he wouldn't win any points. He would have appeared taller, if he hadn't been enveloped in a chunkiness sometimes common to short people.

Fay wondered how long he was going to be unaffected by her presence before he paid her a courtesy call.

"Hello, Fay," he said as he wandered over to the drafting table in the little concrete enclosure that served as a makeshift office for lab supervisors. "How do the entries look?"

"Fine, considering I worked on them all last evening and well into the night."

"I know what you mean." He turned to go as if he recalled something.

"Alan," she began, hesitantly, hating herself for her timidity at that moment. "Why are you avoiding me?"

He looked surprised. "Avoiding you? Why do you say that?"

At once she was struck by a sense of the ridiculous. Here amidst compressors, steam generators, and boilers used in batch filtration and air compression experiments, they were discussing the waning embers of their relationship.

"You know why. You have your answering machine on all the time in your office. You didn't use to." She knew she sounded like a petulant schoolgirl, rather than an employee of the department. Whatever the cause of his behavior, he could at least have been up front. He owed her that.

"I have my machine on when I'm out of the office or with students," he replied, passing a finger lightly over the inside of a glass tube, as if to see if it was dry. Not that the presence of a dry glass tube was imperative. Fay knew he just wanted to avoid looking her in the eye. He was suddenly going clean-cut, the regular guy, the devoted family man. He was overcome by an attack of conscience. Why? He wasn't saying.

"Sure. And I'm the Tsarina of Russia."

"Oh, come on, Fay. Be reasonable." His voice was low, purring with sensuality.

She looked at him, mildly perplexed as to why she found him attractive, even now, with their affair about to fizzle out.

Nick left the lab to get himself the inevitable bagel and cream cheese at the University cafeteria. It was only 8:30 in the morning. The lab classes would start at noon.

Although they were alone for the time being, Fay tried not to appear too eager or infatuated.

"Reasonable about what? That you're avoiding me? You've not had an attack of conscience, have you?" After his promise of divorcing Monica, his new-found conscience seemed misplaced.

"There's no need for sarcasm."

What she really wanted to do was needle him about his wife, Monica, a champion of adult education and battered women in the community. She was a volunteer for Dial Help and spent every opportunity trying to attract potential volunteers to its cause. Fay remembered meeting her at a fall term party for students. She was an energetic woman who floated around the room greeting everyone noisily, "How lovely you look. But you *must* join our group. We need your talent."

Fay noticed with rising contempt that Monica's gregariousness spilled out, enveloping the room like tentacles poised to seize.

"Hello, Miss … er, Harkness," she said, pouncing on Fay. "You must be Alan's lab help. How clever—knowing about all those chemicals." She rambled on, her voice finally trailing off toward the far end of the room, away from the long table weighted down by food.

Fay had just gotten to know Alan. As her supervisor, he had been pleased with the way she kept tabs on the MSDS and worked with the students on the lab experiments. Often they stayed late, working at their respective tasks. On a particularly cold, late evening, he had coffee bubbling in his office and asked her if she would like some. And she accepted.

She knew he liked the way her thick, closely cropped hair fringed her face. He complimented her often. Short and curvaceous …. He once told her he was flattered when she looked at him in that way.

What made her think of all that now? And what did it matter? He wanted her out of his life. So much for a lover's loyalty. A dog's loyalty was worth far more, she thought, as the picture of Norman's golden brown retriever eyes came into her mind and how he would wait for her by the door at five-thirty, when she returned home from work.

Alan moved away from Fay as she got up. "Alan, how soon you've forgotten how it used to be," she said, trying for a disarming gentleness she was far from feeling.

"It had to stop somewhere. You know that." So that meant he had to forget the way she was looking at him, the voluptuousness of her body, her passion. Monica, with her social work, was only a pale, cold facsimile.

The moment snapped like a button for both of them. It was all over—the subterfuge of meeting at strange hours in out-of-the-way motels. How lucky that he hadn't been recognized! He would have been the laughing stock of the university gossip contingent. And Monica's fury! That would have to be seen to be believed.

His voice was soft and avuncular. "It's better this way. You have your work; you're young. I wasn't being fair to you, myself, or Monica."

"What a man!"

He ignored the sarcasm and continued talking to her as if she were a small child. "You'll see. You'll get over this before you know it." He turned to leave. "And please turn off all lights when you leave. No need to leave it to the janitors."

His patronizing manner set her nerves on edge. "Oh, stop being so condescending. You've got something up your sleeve and I mean to find out what it is." She gathered up her purse and stalked off to the women's lounge. She badly needed a cigarette.

The women's lounge was empty. Fay sank into the soft leather couch and, kicking off her moccasins, lay back with her head on the armrest. As she blew out smoke rings and watched them disembody, she began ruminating over the situation between herself and Alan.

Something was up with him. An idea formed in her head. She couldn't get him back, but she was going to give him a few sleepless nights. Fay would tell him that she had a mind to spill the beans to his wife. How would he like that? What did she, Fay, have to lose? They couldn't fire her from her job—her personal life was really none of their business, especially when she was a good employee. Besides that, she had no family here, wasn't married; there was no one she would embarrass.

When Fay finished her cigarette she felt a little better. She emerged from the women's lounge feeling elated, almost powerful. Moreover, she felt benevolent—she could afford to be, because she knew what she was going to do next and Alan didn't.

Fay didn't see Alan again that day. She was in charge of coordinating experiments. As a Research Associate, she was not quite faculty, but a notch above students. Someday, she promised herself, she would go in for a doctorate.

She was alone in the lab with its high ceiling and slag-gray concrete floor. Aluminum step ladders stood in a corner near the entrance to the loading dock, which had a wide, garage-type steel door that was attached to a pulley. Also near the entrance was a wooden ledge with yellow hard hats sitting like little limbless dwarves waiting to be picked up.

The walls were painted a luminous lime yellow, as if, with this almost blinding décor, there would be no possibility that anybody would ever be lulled into a false sense of security.

While waiting for the students to come in, she gathered up appropriate job assessment and evaluation forms to give them as they worked on their experiment in teams. She got out a three-ring binder to serve as an experiment portfolio for each team.

The students came in, each wearing a hard hat, safety goggles, and overshoes.

"Report to your group managers," Fay called.

Air was being fed into a tall cylindrical boiler and compressed at tremendous heat to a dull, persistent hum. Groups of seniors got into formation as two rotors in the cylinder compressed the air. A steel discharge pipe would draw it out into the after-cooler. Where bends in the piping were necessary, flanged fittings with screws lashed them in place. A displaced fitting would result in a misaligned pipe, causing a deadly leak of gas. Since air was being fed continuously, the student groups coming in during the next hour would monitor the experiment.

The main door opened and Nick entered.

"Are you staying?" Fay asked, raising her voice above the sometimes-annoying din in the lab.

"If you like. Do you want me to help supervise?" He had in his hand a sheaf of papers comprising his own report on equipment and changes in policies.

"Would you?"

"Sure. That's all right with me."

Fay liked Nick, who never showed the slightest temperament and was always on hand to cover for her if she was held up inescapably somewhere else. When not working in the lab, monitoring the equipment, he spent hours kayaking in the rapids of Canyon Falls, especially in the late spring. During that time, the water level was high enough to minimize the hazard of hitting rocks and jammed logs. Fay could almost picture him bouncing up and down in his kayak with his yellow and green Windjammer jacket flapping in the wind like a miniature sail.

Fay had taken him under her wing and trained him in his duties. And he didn't seem to resent having a female as his supervisor. She was more than fair. He seldom asked for time off, but when he did, she let him go.

"Do what you have to do. We all have to find our own ways of keeping our sanity around here," she told him once.

Nick's homely face, flowing out of a receding forehead, lit up with a smile each morning. It was all Fay could do to drag herself into the lab office on a cold, unfriendly Monday morning, having gulped down two steaming cups of coffee. If he guessed what was going on between her and Alan in the last year or so, he never let on. He always referred to Alan as "Dr. Kohner."

Nick now hovered around a group of students, assisting them in providing proper grounding while transferring ethanol from a drum to the feed tank. A copper wire was attached to the two receptacles to prevent static electricity.

"There," he said, standing back, pleased with his efforts. "All yours."

"Is Dr. Kohner coming in today?" Fay asked him casually, her eyes on her worksheet, although she was only partially attentive to it.

"I doubt it. He's at a meeting. He's always in meetings, now that he's tipped for Department Chair of Chemical Engineering." Nick fairly yelled as the choking and wheezing of the machines got louder. It was also getting hotter. He wiped his face with a red-and-white bandana, which he had tied around his neck.

"Department Chair?" The thudding inside her head seemed to mark time with the machines in the lab. "I didn't hear about that. When did this come about?"

"Well, there was talk about it at the last meeting. By the way, where were you?"

"I was at the loading zone watching the truck pick up liquid waste."

So that was it! That explained Alan's sudden conversion to devoted family man. He was telling her—and himself—that he hadn't worked hard all these years, bringing in money in research funding, only to throw it all away on a mindless affair.

Fay put her papers away and looked around. The students were absorbed in their work and were on their own. She needed time to think.

"Well, good for him," she said in reply.

"There are outside candidates, I hear, but Dr. Kohner stands a good chance." Then his voice became confidential. "Fay, let me give you a word of advice."

"Yes?" She looked at him, puzzled.

"Leave well alone. The man is a philanderer. Cold and selfish, besides. You're too good for him."

"What do you mean?" How much did he know?

"It isn't difficult to put two and two together, Fay." He didn't seem to want to say too much and Fay liked him for that.

She let out a mirthless laugh. It was almost a relief that Nick knew.

"I actually thought he'd leave Monica someday, but that was before the Grand Prize of Department Chair was dangled before his eyes."

Nick didn't reply. He fidgeted with his papers, shuffling them, as if looking for something. "Tough break, Fay. But it's not the end of the world."

"Yes, I know. Thanks for listening." She patted him on the shoulder

"Sure. Any time."

✗   ✗   ✗   ✗

When Fay drove home around 5:30, it was starting to drizzle—a late fall day. The pelting drops slithered down her face and neck, settling under the inside of the collar of her jacket. She had not worn her hooded jacket, as if willing the bad weather to hold off for a while. But in these parts, that was wishful thinking.

She drove to the familiar row of houses that stood to attention, like well-honed soldiers, on either side of a narrow avenue of maple trees. The leaves were strewn in forlorn disarray on the ground, forming a slippery carpet over brown, cold-deadened grass.

Fay's rented house was dark inside, but from her parking space, she could see Norman at the window, perched up on the armchair, watching her drive up—a young lion surveying his kingdom.

Norman greeted her with tail-wagging fanfare and encircled her feet, coaxing her into playing ball with him on the carpet.

"Did you miss me?" She left her purse, briefcase, and grocery bag on the dining table and picked up the faded tennis ball. "Let's go outside and play for a while. You've been a good boy all day, waiting for momma to come home."

Norman sat on his haunches, his head angled, watching her. Seeing the door open, he jumped up and gamboled onto the yard, not minding the rain-soaked ground a bit.

Fay threw the ball several yards while he ran madly after it, returning it to her, proud of his feat. After ten minutes of this, Norman showed distinct signs of losing interest. He'd had his fill of exercise, now he wanted to go inside and roll on the carpet. As Fay pushed him along lazily with her knee, he looked back at her, as if making sure she was close behind, and trotted back into the house.

✗   ✗   ✗   ✗

It was the following afternoon that Fay saw *him* again, quite by chance. She was at the darkened corridor leading to the Unit Op Lab when he was just emerging from the exit door to the wing that held the faculty offices. There was an awkward pause as she jingled her keys in her jacket pocket.

"Oh, there you are, Fay," he said briskly. "There is a new consignment of reagents coming in sometime this afternoon. Could you enter them in the MSDS as soon as possible?"

"I don't know if I can do it today. I have some lab reports to grade—a stack of them in my office."

"I know, but this is urgent. The reagents have to be entered before tomorrow's experiment."

It is business as usual now, Fay thought. I could be a lab apparatus for all he knows—or cares.

"Nick says you're one of the contenders for Department Chair—congratulations," Fay said, but there was no accompanying congeniality.

"Whoa. I haven't got it yet," he said, laughing. It was the hollow laugh of somebody trying to be informal with a subordinate. How soon the line of demarcation crept up!

"As they say—there is many a slip between the cup and the lip." She deliberately sounded ominous, not knowing why. Just that she couldn't resist the only weapon in her power—of making a remark that sounded like a veiled threat.

He gave her a look that she couldn't fathom—of warning? A sinister message shot through that look, as if to say, "You'd better watch what you're saying."

Fay had an incredible urge to lead him along an eerie path, like an insect being led deeper and deeper into the gossamer web of a spider, each step leading farther into a maze.

"The provost will back your bid for Department Chair. You have an excellent publishing record, administrative skills, and a personal record above reproach."

He listened silently, a muscle working in his cheek. She enjoyed seeing him sweat with anger.

In the next moment his face cleared. "Fay, I was wrong." His tone was conciliatory. "I'd like to see you again." He moved toward her, his body taut, but on his face was a smile calculated to bring back the feelings that were lost between them.

Fay took a step back, as if recoiling from the sting of a viper. "No, Alan. I guess you were right all along. It's over. We were doing ourselves more harm than anything else."

She glanced at her watch hurriedly. "Oh, look at the time. I'll come back at night to do the reagents." She had the satisfaction of leaving him puzzled as she walked to the end of the corridor and turned into a small cubicle with a half-door through which she entered her office.

On her desk was a pile of folders containing lab reports. These she put into an oversized shoulder bag. She would finish these at home and return later to enter the reagents. Fay smirked to herself; she was getting better and better at shucking off Alan. Why was he attempting to get back together?

She gathered up her keys and went into the parking lot.

✗   ✗   ✗   ✗

Norman was not there to greet her as she let herself into the house, still and quiet in the dwindling late afternoon sunlight.

"Norman," she called, "here boy."

But there was no sign of the loping retriever who usually greeted her with vigorous tail-wagging attention.

She found him in her study curled on the gray shag rug in the middle of the room. Seeing her enter, he arose and walked toward her with a limp.

"What is it, Norman? Here, let me see." Pulling him down into her lap she picked up his right paw and scrutinized it. It was bleeding and swollen. "You poor baby! When could this have happened? Yesterday, in the yard?" There must have been shards of glass under the deceptively even carpet of leaves.

She tore out a piece of gauze and bandaged it. "Easy, boy." He whined a little and looked up sadly at her.

Fay called the emergency number at the vet's clinic. Yes, they would see him, but could she come in another hour since they were tied up with a hit-and-run case? She felt herself go slack with despair as she thought of the MSDS that had to be updated. She'd just have to ask Nick to go in for her.

An hour and a half later, she was at the clinic. A med tech cleaned out Norman's wound. The cut was deep and there was still a piece of glass in it, but she removed the shard and bandaged it up again.

It was close on ten o'clock and Fay didn't want to leave Norman by himself.

She decided to treat Nick to dinner as a thank-you gesture for doing the MSDS for her.

✗   ✗   ✗   ✗

It was the following morning that she learnt that her plan of treating Nick to dinner would be out of the question.

There was a crowd of people outside the Van Clement building, as well as the sheriff's van and an ambulance with the flashing beam alarmingly absent. Students hovered, some with their hands covering their faces in horror. Fay approached them cautiously, her head pounding. A yellow plastic tape cordoned off the area, an alarm was shrieking somewhere in the building, probably the basement which housed the labs.

"What happened?" she asked one of the janitors she recognized.

"Nick Schulte. He died. An accident in the lab."

"What!" Fay felt her stomach churn. It was her fault. *No, no.* He had subbed for her before.

"But how did it happen?" She pulled at the sleeve of a policeman.

"There was a leak. Nitrogen gas."

Fay moved to the back silently and looked around. Among a group consisting of policemen, campus Public Safety and university officials was Alan. When he saw her approach he looked at her as if he had seen a ghost.

"Fay," he said in a whisper. "I thought you were going to do the updates. Where were you?"

"I couldn't. Norman had an accident and I had to take him to the vet."

"Norman? Your dog?" He nearly exploded as his whisper got more fierce. "Do you realize a man is dead? Maybe he accidently touched something."

"Accidently touched something, Alan?" Fay said in a deliberately smooth tone of voice. "Nick was not a novice. He knew what he was doing."

She glanced at him obliquely as a thought flashed in her mind. *He expected her to be there.* Was she the intended victim? He inspected lab equipment. He knew all about pipings and fittings, how they worked—and how they went out of order. *How they leaked to let out nitrogen gas—odorless, colorless nitrogen.*

She had to get out of his orbit, fast. She moved toward a knot of people, wanting to be alone to think, to absorb what happened and maybe make sense of her fears.

Fay stood there numb, watching. All she had were her suspicions to go by. And what help were they? From her vantage point she saw Alan talking to a university official, then a police officer.

Moments later, the officer was walking toward her. "I'm Deputy Sheriff Vignali," he said. "May I ask you a few questions? Let's go into the van."

He pushed opened the door of the white police van and stood aside for Fay to get in. Leaning against the door, he took out a steno pad and a pen. "Dr. Kohner says you're in charge of the lab."

So Alan set Deputy Vignali on her trail and as far away from himself as possible. "In a manner of speaking, yes."

"What do you do?"

"Set up and supervise lab experiments. Grade lab reports."

"You work closely with Dr. Kohner?"

"Both Nick and I did."

"Where were you last night?"

"I was supposed to do the updates, but my dog had to be taken to the vet, so I asked Nick to cover for me."

"An unfortunate switch," Vignali said.

"It might have been me," Fay said. If the business of their affair came out, so be it. If Alan were ever brought to justice, it would, anyway.

"Did Dr. Kohner know you couldn't make it?"

"I don't think so."

Vignali was silent. He appeared to be thinking. "So you were not in this vicinity at all?"

"No." She felt herself go slack from relief. By pointing a finger in her direction, Alan was implying there was carelessness on her part. Not likely. She followed regulations closely.

"When we can go in there, I'd like you to accompany me. Do you mind?"

"Wouldn't Dr. Kohner be better?" Fay asked.

"We'll be questioning him, too. But he suggested you. He thinks highly of you. Said you were a good worker."

Fay said nothing. A picture was evolving. Of Alan trying to keep his hands and nose clean while a verdict of "accidental death" was being enacted.

Hours later, they stood in the gray light of the lab. The light was turned off. Fay raised her hand to switch on the light.

"No," Vignali said. "Don't turn it on. Everything has been left as it was since last night. Do you see, ma'am?"

Fay looked at him, puzzled.

"The light was off last night. If the victim had been working, he'd have been found with the light left on. But somebody turned it off. Turns out the security camera was turned off at nine, an hour before the time of death." Vignali stopped to take a breath. "Who manages the security camera?"

"None of us are allowed to touch it."

"That leaves Dr. Kohner."

"He is a stickler for turning off non-essential lights and systems." *And a penny-pinching so-and-so.*

"This puts a different angle on things." Vignali turned on the light and looked around. A muscle tensed in his jaw. "It's serious that somebody turned off the light and the camera. Does Dr. Kohner work late every day?"

"Yes."

"His fingerprints will probably be the only ones on the camera." He looked up at it, sitting on a ledge near the entrance, and then around him. "Some setup you have here. Is that the pipe that compresses air?" He walked over to it. "What's this?" He took out a pair of tweezers and picked up a folded piece of paper by the edge and shook it out. "Looks like a list of meetings of some sort. With scribbles on it." He held it out to Fay.

It was a list of candidates interviewing for the position of department chair and the timings. Alan probably had it handy to study the competition. "These people are in the running for department chairman. So is Dr. Kohner. The doodles are in his handwriting."

Vignali dangled the paper above a Ziploc bag, dropped it in, and sealed it. "We'll fingerprint it."

Now there was a little more than suspicions. Vignali was kindly in his manner and Fay felt almost light-headed with relief.

"Are you okay?"

"If there's nothing else …."

"Of course." He walked with her into the hallway. "I have to tell you, it doesn't look good for Dr. Kohner. Now," he said, "suppose you tell me what your relationship with him was?"

Here it comes. "We were lovers and he broke it off. I threatened to spill the beans to his wife. Don't ask me why," Fay said with a grimace.

"I have to tell you, I lied when I said he spoke highly of you. He said you were careless with your work and opinionated. But that didn't jibe with what I heard from some of the others. I had my suspicions." He gave her a wry smile.

Fay stared at him, trying to take in what he said. "Thank you," she said at last. "Now may I have that ride home?"

✗

Rekha Ambardar has published over one hundred short genre and mainstream stories, articles, and essays in print and electronic magazines, including *The Writer's Journal*, *ByLine*, *The Indian Express*, and *Writing World.com*. Her mysteries have been published in *Futures*, *Nefarious*, *The Gumshoe Review*, *Orchard Mystery Press*, *Shots in the Dark*, and other anthologies. She is also the author of two romance novels.

CONDUCT UNBECOMING

by Robert Knightly

He sat across the desk from the other man, but whose face he could not see because it was in the shadows. The only light came from a desk lamp, and the shade on the single window was drawn. The other wore a business suit and tie, while he was in uniform: the regulation summer blouse, his insignia of sergeant's rank properly affixed to the sleeves, as were his service stripes, the five black bands signifying twenty-five years of service in the city's police department. He didn't know where he was or how he'd gotten there, but he wore no gun belt under the blouse, nor did he have his holstered off-duty revolver tucked inside his belt, riding in the comfortable pocket made by his right hip where it met his waist. He was weaponless.

"Smoke if you got 'em, Sergeant," the other said, remaining motionless in his chair. It was positioned aslant so he could not see the other's face at all. The suggestion startled him; he had not thought to want a cigarette till the other mentioned it, although he'd been a smoker for most of his life.

"What the hell is this? Where am I?" he demanded. Voicing his anger kept at bay the dread building within him.

"You're here for adjudication of charges and specifications, Sergeant," the other stated matter-of-factly. "For reconciliation," he added after a pause.

"For what? I've got twenty-eight years in the job and never a complaint, never a reprimand!"

"Specification One: Conduct Unbecoming an Officer and Prejudicial to the Good Order and Discipline of the Department," the other droned. "Specification Two: Negligent Failure to Be Fit for Duty."

"That's bullshit! Where's my lawyer? Aren't I entitled to a lawyer, like the worst skel in the street?"

"This is an informal procedure, Sergeant. Those rules don't apply here."

Suddenly, the other reached out and depressed the button on an oblong silver-and-black cassette recorder that sat squarely on the desk between them. The sergeant recognized the machine, the kind he'd used himself, the kind that every detective used to record confessions in every interrogation room in every squad in the city.

"He wouldn't leave, you know," the woman's voice said clearly, filling the room. "I begged him … for me, for the kids, for himself, before it was too late, before there was nothing left to save, but he wouldn't listen. He just couldn't leave now he'd say, not just yet but later he would, he'd say."

"Gloria? That you?" He stared at the recorder as the disembodied voice of his wife continued.

"Twenty-eight years playing second fiddle to the damn job! The department always came first, before all of us, me, the kids, no matter what. He was a detective then, our youngest was graduating from high school and I wanted us to be there for her, I begged him. But no-o-o!" The voice broke, bitter. "He was on a case, couldn't get away, twenty years and more he was on one case or another and could never get away … I just couldn't live with it another day …" The other man stopped the tape.

"She left me, took the kids," he said, then wrenching his gaze from the recorder, appealed to the other who sat, a faceless, silent accuser, not ten feet away. "What could I do? It's the job. You're a detective, you stay with a case day-in-day-out, where it leads you follow and when it breaks you got to be there … No choice, there was never a choice."

The other reached across the desk and depressed the 'play' button again.

"He lived the job," a male voice said, in a flat Queens accent.

"Jerry? That you, Jerry?" he interrupted, but the voice continued.

"He went off the deep end with the missing kid. The case was in the papers, it dragged on for years. One day a six-year-old named Jason goes off to school by himself—the poor dumb mother actually thinks you can let a little kid walk to school by himself. Poof! Disappears, not a trace. Nada. Him and me, we catch the case, bust our humps on it month after month …" The voice paused, as if remembering. "Eventually, I give up, the department gives up, even the parents want to give up, I think, but no way; he won't let them. Because he knows the kid's alive. He can feel him near! That's what he tells them."

"I could!" he yelled at the recorder, almost launching himself from his chair. "I could," he whispered.

"Bananas!" the voice continued. "He went south on that one. Worked on his own time, month after month, year after year, running down leads, will-o-the-wisps, like a cat chasing its tail. Jesus!" The voice paused, then reanimated, plunged on. "Got himself leather and a motorcycle, hung out with a biker gang on East Fourth Street, was sure the kid was somewhere nearby. Felt it, he said. I hoped making rank, getting promoted, would cure him. Putting on the bag again, going back to patrol as a boss, not a peon any more. Then he'd call to tell me how it was. A fish out of water; it was different but not better. Now he worried about the young cops in his squad, worried about not being able to teach them what they needed to know, worried sick about making a mistake, screwing up royally, so bad that he'd get them hurt or lose the job, blow the pension. When he took off the uniform, went home, it all went with him—" The man stopped the tape.

"Shove it, Jerry!" he shouted, staring at the recorder. "Tell me that when you have five kids and a wife yelling she's leaving you if you don't pack in the job—a thing you've loved, that's understood and taken care of you all your life since you became a man. 'Me or them', she says. 'That job is killing you.' A lot she knew. The job was my life! I'm a cop, that's what I do, what I am. Sure, retire? A high school graduate, retire to what?" He paused, staring at the shadowed, silent witness, as if awaiting his response. The other's hand moved to the recorder again, depressing a button.

"I found him." The strong, young female voice filled the room. "When I got off the midnight tour, I went straight home that morning as usual. Not finding him in the house, I went out to the garage where he liked to work on his motorcycle. That's where he was, lying by the workbench, his service gun still in his hand, dressed in his uniform like he was going to work. I don't think I'll ever be able to forgive him … Oh, Daddy!" She choked back a sob.

He listened dully to the voice of his daughter, then came to life, exclaimed in anguish: "Oh, sweetheart! Baby! It had to be you, don't you see? The only other cop in the family, the only one strong enough to …" He halted, searching for just the right words.

"I was in a box, no way out. But I couldn't let strangers find me, not like that." As he spoke from the heart, his hand rose to the right side of his head, fingers caressing the contours of the crater where his right temple had been.

Just then, the other leaned into the pool of the lamplight, exposing his face and his right profile—what was left of it. With a start, the sergeant recognized the dapper boss whom he, as a rookie detective, had worked for so long ago. A detective-lieutenant who, on the eve of his subpoenaed appearance before a grand jury investigating police corruption, had laid out his personal effects on the desk in his squad-room office—lieutenant's shield, ID card, keys, wallet containing snapshots of the family—then gone into a stall in the precinct washroom and shot himself with his service revolver.

"Do you feel Jason near, Sergeant?" he asked, sitting back in his chair so that his head and upper torso were again swallowed by the darkness.

Jolted as if by a live wire, the sergeant stood, knocking over the chair he'd been sitting on. "Where?" he demanded, his head swiveling wildly back and forth, trying in vain to see into the blacked-out reaches of the room. "Give him up, he's mine!" he cried, unheeded.

✗

Robert Knightly retired from the NYPD as a Lieutenant, then was a trial lawyer in the Criminal Division of the NYC Legal Aid Society. Author of two police procedural novels from Severn House; editor of *Queens Noir*, Akashic Books, and published short stories in *Brooklyn Noir*, *Manhattan Noir*, and *Brooklyn Noir 3*.

SPIRIT OF THE LAW

by Jacqueline Seewald

"**H**e's dead."

"Who's dead?"

The woman on the other end of the phone began to sob.

"Mary, is that you?"

"Yes." Her voice had a child-like quality. "It's K. He's dead. I need your help."

I did my best to calm her. Mary Logan lived with Randall Kaminowski for a number of years. She was devoted to him. She was also not the most together woman I'd ever met. I would have to describe her as fragile.

"Where are you?"

"At the house."

Dumb question on my part. Where else would she be? Mary was more housekeeper than girlfriend. As I understood it, she and K had been sweethearts back in high school. They'd gone their separate ways and years later, after both had been divorced, they'd rekindled their friendship. Mary, although she had grown children on the West Coast, chose to move in with K in his New Jersey house. The arrangement seemed to work well for both of them.

"Where is he?"

This brought a fresh round of sobs.

"Mary, please, I need to know what happened if I'm going to help you. Take a deep breath and let it out slowly. Good. Now explain what happened."

She did as I asked. "Tom, the police, they said he killed himself right there in his office."

I found it hard to believe that K would do such a thing. Sure, of late things hadn't been going well for him in his business, but in my opinion K loved life too much to end it intentionally.

"I'll find out what's going on," I promised. "If you've got tranquilizers, now might be a good time to take one."

"Please call as soon as you know anything more."

The phone call ended and I stared straight ahead without really seeing much of anything. K had been one of my first clients. I really liked the guy, in spite of the fact that for a man in his late fifties he behaved more like an out-of-control teenager than a mature adult. Here I was not even thirty yet, having to constantly offer advice to a man almost twice my age. But K was nothing like my own father, who was always critical of me. K valued my thoughts and opinions.

The day I first met K, the phone rang only twice in my office—a wrong number and someone soliciting. I got really sick of sitting at my desk and staring at the ugly wallpaper and carpeting. At five p.m., I walked over to Finnegan's Bar where Happy Hour included free food. A bunch of lawyers hung out there and I did a little networking since the place is like a New Jersey version of Cheers. The watering hole was packed with businessmen. I passed out my cards. Hope springs eternal, according to the poet.

In a little while, a big burly man approached me. He was staring at my card, looking me up and down. "Says here you do criminal and civil work. I'm kind of in a bind."

"Tell me about your problem." We took a private booth way in the back. I chose the gunfighter's seat. I wasn't worried about being shot in the back—Finnegan's isn't that kind of place, but I do like having a full view of the establishment.

K and I ordered drinks. K told me he owned a large construction company. As we talked, I realized he had smarts. Eventually, K explained why he needed a defense attorney. He sometimes drank and drove. A really bad combination.

As his attorney for the past year, I represented him in two D.W.I. cases and a lawsuit. But that wasn't the worst of his problems. The Feds were leaning on him to help bring down mobster Anthony Alfonso, known in some circles as Tony the Terrorist, a made man who no one who had common sense would mess with. But like Einstein said, common sense is not so common.

I knew K was emotionally upset when he'd come to my office to tell me about this latest predicament—nobody came to my place of business unless forced. Usually, I would visit K at his office.

"They want me to wear a wire. Can you believe that? Tom, you're my lawyer. What do you think I should do?" K's face reddened, reminding me of a slab of rare roast beef.

"Are you satisfied with the will I drew up for you?"

K ran his right hand through his shock of graying hair. "Not funny."

"Didn't mean it to be."

K tented his long fingers. "There are some changes I want to make in my will. But that can wait until we figure out how to handle this crisis."

"If you do what the Feds ask, you'll piss off Tony the Terrorist. He's got a reputation for whacking people for a lot less."

"Tell me about it. But, Tom, if I don't cooperate, they'll go after me. They're threatening to shut down my business. If they do that, I'll starve."

I sat back in my chair and studied K. In the short time I'd known him, the man had deteriorated. His eyes were bloodshot, likely from lack of sleep or heavy drinking or self-medicating—probably all three.

"Look, I've represented you before. Remember that nasty lawsuit? You stayed in business. It'll be okay."

K bit down on his lower lip. "But you can't really be sure of that."

I could have said he should never have gotten involved with Tony. But K was a weak man and he'd told me that when Tony's lieutenants approached him initially, they'd made him an offer he didn't feel comfortable refusing. It wasn't my place to judge K. My job was to represent him when he needed an attorney.

✗　　✗　　✗　　✗

Lara Lopez entered my office, drawing my mind back to the present moment. Lara smiled at me, bringing a whiff of spring with her. She was a tall, slim young woman with long, shiny black hair and deep dark eyes. Her skin was olive and her high cheekbones denoting her Chilean heritage.

"How's school?" I asked her.

She shrugged. "Same as usual. I have to prepare for exams. Do you have some work for me to do today?" She had only a slight accent.

"A couple of letters to type, nothing pressing."

She smiled like a madonna. "I suppose that's both good and bad."

I turned my head from side to side. "Business could be better. Wish I could afford to pay you more."

Lara sat down at the second battered desk in my shabby office. The blue wallpaper had faded and peeled. Someone had ground chewing gum into the worn gray carpet. A single narrow window offered a view of a brick wall and a dirty alley. My mother's amateur landscape paintings had been hung on the walls in strategic locations to hide the cracks. The best that could be said about my office was that the rent was affordable and it was a block away from the courthouse.

"I have my fellowship money. It covers all my expenses. Besides, you need me."

We both knew that was true. The day I met Lara, both of us studying side by side on computers at the university library, was one of the better days of my life. Even though I'd done a stretch in the Marine Corps and then worked for a while at a big firm in Manhattan, I wasn't the most organized of people. Lara was. When her fellowship ended and she was forced to go back to Chile, I would really miss her. I'd have liked to deepen our relationship, but in reality I had little to offer. I was a single practitioner struggling to establish my own small law firm. I wanted to keep working independently and be my own boss. Trouble was there were too many lawyers in New Jersey for the amount of work available.

"I found out today that Mr. K is dead."

Lara looked up from the computer she'd just started to boot up. "I'm very sorry to hear that. He was a nice man." Of course, K tried to flirt with Lara. Who could blame him? He'd invited Lara and me for a steak dinner one evening and taken us to an expensive restaurant. He'd been quite taken with Lara.

"The thing is, Mary says the police called her and said K committed suicide."

Lara frowned. "That surprises me."

"He was really stressed the last time we spoke."

Lara tapped a pen against the hard wood desk in a thoughtful manner. "He did not strike me as a man of courage. I believe it takes a certain amount of courage to end one's life."

I paid attention to what Lara said. She had a Master's degree in psychology, had worked as a prison psychologist in her own country, and was studying for a Ph.D. in clinical psychology at the university. If I ever got an important jury trial, Lara was the one person I'd want as a consultant to help me select a jury.

"As K's attorney and the executor of his will, I'll have a lot to do."

"Perhaps you should look into the manner of his death." Lara raised her dark brows.

"That's a job for the police," I said.

Lara shrugged. "You might want to make certain that he truly died by his own hand. Sometimes, appearances are deceiving."

"I'm a lawyer, not a detective, Lara."

"A bit cold, don't you think? He was your friend as well as a client."

I shrugged. What Lara said was true. "All right, I'll talk to the cops. Pull K's will from his file. I'll check out the beneficiaries."

✗   ✗   ✗   ✗

While Lara fixed fresh coffee, I studied K's will. I knew K spent money lavishly when he had it and even when he didn't. He'd been pretty well cleaned out. His first two wives had been well off in their own rights. Wife number one was a successful interior designer. Wife number two lived off a large inheritance. No children from either marriage. He'd had two children by the third wife, though. She was the one who'd demanded heavy assets during his best earning years. She'd claimed she was disabled and couldn't work, that K needed to support her. He'd paid alimony and child support for many years. I gathered the marriage ended bitterly because K had been a womanizer and his wife found out he'd cheated on her. He named as his heirs his two daughters who he hadn't seen in nearly fifteen years, as well as Mary Logan. For a man who'd once been very prosperous, his only assets appeared to be his heavily-mortgaged house and a couple of small bank accounts. His business was in bad financial shape, teetering toward bankruptcy. I observed that partnering with Tony the Terrorist had not made matters better for him—just the reverse.

Lieutenant Monroe wasn't in a talkative mood. "Atkins, your client overdosed," he said, as if that ended the matter.

"Hard to believe. Was there a suicide note?"

Monroe narrowed his thin lips as if he were sucking on a lemon. Dealing with this cop was not pleasant. "We don't have the M.E.'s report yet."

"I'm the executor of Mr. K's will. Can I get the information as soon as it's available? I'll need it for the family."

He cursed me under his breath as I started to leave the office.

✗ ✗ ✗ ✗

As it turned out, there was no suicide note. However, K apparently ingested a large quantity of alcohol. The toxicology report determined there was a massive amount of insulin in the alcohol, an oral insulin drug that caused prolonged hypoglycemia. In layman's language, K slipped into a coma and never woke up. He'd waited until everyone in the office left for the day, sat down at his desk and drunk himself into oblivion. K was a diabetic, so no surprise that he would have access to the drug.

"Case closed," Lieutenant Monroe said, after sharing this information with me over the phone.

Monroe was probably right. So why did I feel there was something more to this? I guess because what Lara said got me thinking. I wasn't an intuitive person, but I had known K pretty well. No matter how upset he'd been, it just didn't seem like something he would do to himself. Sure he could behave bi-polar at times but he wasn't crazy, just emotionally stunted. K had grown up as the only child of older parents. They were wealthy and doting. From what he'd told me about himself, K had been a self-centered child. His mother was overly indulgent. He hadn't liked school and rebelled against rules. His father took him into his construction business and K did well. Trouble was K had been spoiled rotten as a child, according to his own account, and remained immature and ego-centric. He was the center of a universe that revolved around him.

I handled the arrangements for K's funeral. I decided on a graveside service instead of a chapel. I knew only a few people would be present. I drove Mary, who was in no shape to drive a vehicle herself. Several of K's employees came to pay last respects. A well-dressed, attractive older woman wept during the short service. I wondered who she was.

Afterwards, I took Mary's arm, seated her in the passenger seat of my Toyota and went over to the mystery woman before she could take off in her own car.

"Hi, I'm Tom Atkins, K's attorney, or at least I was his lawyer."

The woman smiled tremulously, her blue eyes watery. "Yes, I know who you are. Randall spoke of you. I believe he thought of you as a substitute son."

"And you are?"

"Jessica Wheeler. I was his friend. As a matter of fact, we were talking about making a serious commitment to each other. I'm heartbroken." She dabbed at her eyes with a tissue.

"I'm sorry for your loss," I said, not knowing what else to say except to fall back on trite words.

She hurried away and I confessed to feeling relieved. I still had to deal with Mary, though. She talked nonstop in a disjointed manner as I drove. I didn't interrupt. I couldn't help wondering if K kept Jessica Wheeler and Mary Logan from knowing about each other. It seemed likely.

✗　✗　✗　✗

I held the reading of the will with the heirs on the following Sunday. I was embarrassed to invite them to my shabby office and so arranged with another attorney whose overflow work I often handled *per diem* to use his conference room. I appreciated the favor and would pay him back. Lara came soon after I did and got ready to take notes she would later transcribe.

K's daughters arrived together, both dressed conservatively. They hadn't attended the funeral. I observed that neither daughter kept their father's last name. They were Sarah Granger and Corinne Ellis. I didn't ask if they were married, since it wasn't any of my business. Sarah was two years older than her sister and several inches taller. They were in their late twenties, slender and fair.

Neither much resembled K. They were polite but distant. Mary showed up shortly after the sisters.

After we were all scatcd around the conference table, I passed out copies of the will.

"I'm surprised he left us anything," Sarah observed. "He wasn't much of a father. His work always came first. We hardly saw him. Then after he and Mom split up, we didn't see him at all. Of course we left New Jersey and moved to Maryland to live with Mom's parents."

Corinne licked dry lips. "I think he was involved with another woman. That's what I overheard them fighting about before Mom took us and left him."

I didn't comment. Instead, I began reading aloud the terms of K's last will and testament. To Sarah, K left his art collection. I informed her that K had some good oil paintings. To Corinne, K left his antique toy collection. I explained that these had considerable value as well. The sisters agreed that they would accept what had been left to them in their father's will and we made appropriate arrangements.

"It doesn't make up for the years of neglect," Sarah remarked, "but Corinne and I can use whatever money his things will bring." Her tone of voice could have frozen a desert.

After the sisters left, I turned to Mary, who leaned forward in her chair.

I continued to read. "For Mary Logan, my good friend, I leave my home."

She gave a quick nod.

"Mary, I'm sorry to tell say you that won't be able to keep the house."

Her eyes opened wide. Her face reddened. "He said I was to have the house. He put it in his will." She pointed.

"K was in debt. The house was heavily mortgaged. He'd fallen behind on his payments."

"He never could manage money. He always spent more than he earned." She ripped at a tissue, her manner agitated.

"So you understand why we have to sell the house? Without K's income, it would end up being taken over by the bank. You'd get nothing if they foreclosed on the house. If we sell as quickly as possible, you'll receive whatever money there is after his debts are paid. There's also the furnishings. They're yours, too."

"What about his bank accounts?" She tossed me a hard look.

"There isn't much. They go to pay his funeral expenses and debts."

She nodded again, tears now flowing freely. "He was such a fool. He had everything and threw it all away, and for what?" She looked from me to Lara.

I wasn't certain what Mary meant, but I had a sudden, awful inkling. I hated to confront her at a time like this, and yet it seemed necessary.

"Did K tell you about his relationship with Jessica Wheeler?"

The woman lowered her head and wouldn't meet my eyes. She didn't answer. Old as she was, Mary Logan looked like a little girl caught cheating on a test. Then she glanced up with a sudden hard stare.

"Don't judge me," she shouted, her face flushing again, tone defiant. "You don't have the right."

I exchanged a meaningful look with Lara. I believed she had similar thoughts to mine.

"What don't I understand?"

"He asked me to leave. Can you imagine that? The old fool had himself a new girlfriend, at his age. He was thinking of marrying her, bringing her into our house and kicking me out. He was even talking about changing his will. Said he wasn't happy with his life."

"So you decided to add something to his liquor? Something to help him into the next world before he got a chance to change his will? Maybe you hoped Anthony Alfonso and his gang might be blamed for K's death. But that isn't Tony's way. His hits are strictly gangland style. You were lucky the cops decided K committed suicide."

"I didn't mean to kill him. He drove me crazy." She turned a pleading look toward Lara. "You understand, don't you? He was so selfish. I did everything for that man for so many years. How could he?" Mary buried her face in her hands.

I couldn't answer her question. Maybe Lara might be able to do so. What I did know was that it would be necessary to put in another call to Lieutenant Monroe and I wasn't looking forward to that.

✗

Multiple award-winning author, Jacqueline (J.P.) Seewald, has taught creative, expository, and technical writing at Rutgers University as well as high school English. She also worked as both an academic librarian and an educational media specialist. Fifteen of her books of fiction have been published to critical praise including books for adults, teens, and children. Her short stories, poems, essays, reviews, and articles have appeared in hundreds of diverse publications and numerous anthologies such as: *The Writer*, *L.A. Times*, *Reader's Digest*, *Pedestal*, *Sherlock Holmes Mystery Magazine*, *Over My Dead Body!*, *Gumshoe Review*, *The Mystery Megapack*, *Library Journal*, and *Publishers Weekly*.

PACT

by Dave Beynon

"You need to see this to believe it."

Chester had come up to meet me at the door. His face was a mask of sweat and grime. His hair sported flecks of ancient mortar. Lime dust and calcium billowed from his clothes with each step. Clapping my shoulder, he left a grey palm print on my jacket. I knew from the look on his face that he'd found what we were looking for but I had to ask the question.

"From the look of you, you got through that wall. Is it there?"

"Oh," he said, his eyes wide, "it's there, all right. But ..."

But? I was losing my patience. I'd been on site all day and had left to get a few hours's sleep at the Guesthaus in the village. I had no idea how thick the wall was, or even if the walled-up remnants of the tunnel we were excavating was heading in the right direction. I'd assumed that Chester's night of digging would prove as fruitless as my day had been. My eyes had just closed when my cell phone chirped with Chester's frenzied call telling me to return.

"But what?" I steered him through the arched doorway into what was left of the bombed-out cathedral. "It's either there or it isn't. Which is it?"

"It is there. But there's something in there with it."

"Something?"

"Really," he said, guiding me to the hole we'd made in the floor last week that lead to the narrow stone staircase we'd discovered. "I want you to see this yourself. You're not going to believe it."

"Jesus," I muttered as I took the propane lantern and began to descend.

This particular church had been built in 1236, if the chiselled Roman numerals on the cornerstone could be believed. The Chapel of Saint Agrippina stood just outside this unassuming German hamlet for over seven hundred years before an errant British bomb had all but levelled it toward the end of World War II. Unlike many of the churches destroyed during the war, the Vatican had never seen fit to restore the bricks and mortar of Saint Agrippina's. The villagers below were bewildered by the decision—they had been for three generations—but I knew exactly why Rome was content to leave the church in ruins.

The steps spiralled lazily to the left and I shuffled awkwardly down them, keeping one eye on the orange extension cord at my feet, always snaking deeper into the darkness. The farther I advanced down that staircase the more I felt the damp. During the day it wasn't so bad, but the coolness of the night left the stone walls around me with a chilled layer of sweat.

The stairs finally emptied into what we had been referring to for the last three days as "The Ante-Chamber." The room was about nine feet by seventeen. The east wall was comprised of natural stone. The other three were ancient limestone blocks of varying sizes held together by crumbling mortar trowelled into place by hands over seven hundred years dead. Heaped against the east wall were the blocks and debris of the last three days's work. The excavation of the filled-in passageway we had discovered in the north wall had been slow, tedious work in the tight quarters, but now Chester had broken through. All of this was illuminated in the glaring halogens of a pair of yellow and black pedestal lamps.

"So?" I asked over my shoulder.

Chester's voice was right behind my ear. "Just look."

I adjusted the knob on my lantern, allowing a little more gas at the mantles. I was rewarded with a blast of light to rival the halogens. I walked the length of the room to the northern wall and stepped into the crevice, holding my lantern high. The hissing light chased away the shadows, revealing a circular room beyond.

"Jesus."

The word left my lips as I took in the sight.

The room was forty feet in diameter. The walls narrowed as they rose to what was presumably a dome far above, but this detail was lost to shadow. Halfway along the rough, curved wall there stood a second arched doorway. Where our arch had been walled up with chiselled limestone blocks and mortar, the one opposite was sealed with factory-fired orange brick. In the middle of the room sat the object of our search.

The chest was exactly as described. It was made of tar-coated oak, bound by iron bands and hand-hammered rivets. Encasing it entirely were dozens of yards of weighty, rusted chain. Everything was as documented in The Book.

Only there was a surprise.

Something, slick, leathery and grey, was sitting on top of the chest, one knobby, scarred shoulder raised to shield its eyes from my light.

I let out a breath and the shoulder shifted a fraction. Backing out of the archway, I returned to the Ante-Chamber. Chester looked like a child on Christmas morning.

"So?" He seemed delighted. "What do you think?"

"What do I think?" I turned down the feed on the lantern and placed it on the uneven flagstone floor. "I think we obviously missed something. Run back down to my room at the Guesthaus and get The Book."

"But this is amazing, Roger—"

"You know, Chester, under other circumstances I might be excited about this, but not now. This is … this is an inconvenience we can't really afford. Go get The Book."

Chester pulled a flashlight from his jacket pocket and started for the stairs. His foot lighted on the first step and he turned.

"I'll be back in ten minutes," he said. "What … what are you thinking of doing while I'm gone?"

"Get back as fast as you can. I'm going to see if it can talk."

Chester threw me a doubtful look, then darted up the stairs.

Leaving the lantern on its second lowest setting, I returned to what The Book referred to as The Relic Room. I stopped within the arch and knelt down, the palm of my left hand pressing against the damp stone floor. A foot away from my fingertips I saw what I had expected and feared. Scraped into the surface of the flagstone was an arcane symbol I couldn't immediately interpret, but the mere presence of such a thing was enough to piss me off.

"Damn it," I muttered. My eyes shot up and I instinctively flinched as I registered movement from the middle of the room. With the dimmer light, the shoulder had been lowered, the head thrust forward and a pair of pale yellow eyes regarded me with what looked like mild interest.

"So," I said, addressing the thing that squatted atop the chest, "what the hell am I going to do about you?"

I had little hope it was even capable of understanding me. I had seen something like it once in Yugoslavia, back when it was still called Yugoslavia. That thing had been a mindless, vicious creature, knowing only hunger and bloodshed. It roamed the countryside for weeks. By the time I made it on scene, the monster's rampage had cost twenty-seven people their lives. In the end I'd managed to catch the thing and cage it.

The one who stood before me now was already caged.

"We have a problem here, you and I." I could hear it breathing, a low, burbling rasp. The eyes stared at me as I rose to my feet and fully entered the Relic Room, keeping my back close to the wall. Its body shifted to track me as I travelled the perimeter of the chamber. I paused now and then to examine the etched symbols on the flagstones spaced at regular intervals along the way. Some were familiar, most were not. I really needed Chester to be back with that book.

I arrived at the bricked-up archway and turned my back on the thing to examine it. My fingertips ran along pitted orange brick and plucked a loose bit of mortar that came crumbling off without much coaxing. The texture of this mortar was far different from the stuff we had been chipping through for the last few days.

It felt less substantial—decidedly more modern.

I turned once more to face those unblinking yellow eyes.

"This is shaping up to be a huge pain in the ass for me."

"Imagine how I must feel," the creature replied in a low, whispery voice, "sitting on this rusty chain for all eternity."

I lifted the lantern higher. Up rose the shoulder and a heavily muscled arm, but not enough to cover the eyes. "So it does speak … and has a sense of humor, to boot."

"In a place such as this it helps to keep one's humor."

"I suppose it does. What may I call you?"

"Anything but my true name. How does one address you?"

"Everyone calls me Roger."

"I see. I see. Roger. Roger. Roger." The creature spoke my name like it was trying to decide if it liked the taste of it. "Not a hint of power in a name like that. Obviously not your true and secret name, is it now, Roger?"

I smiled. I'd heard that sometimes they could talk, but had never imagined they could carry on a conversation. "That's what they call me. Care to throw out a name I can call you?"

"They used to call me Bashir. Give it a try. You'll see there's no power to that name, either, but it is one I'll answer to."

With my back to the bricks, I slid into a seated position and placed the lantern on the floor next to me. I reached into my jacket pocket and pulled out a package of cigarettes. I pulled one from the pack, tapped it against my thigh and struck a match. I paused as I brought the flame to the end of the cigarette.

"You don't mind, do you?" I asked, meeting the steady gaze of its eyes over the flickering flame of the match.

"They're your lungs," Bashir said with a shrug, rearranging itself into a cross-legged position on the chest. "You fellows certainly took your time getting here."

I took a deep drag and let it whistle through my teeth. "What do you mean?"

"I've heard you rattling around up there for the past week. And your tunnelling…could you have gone any slower?"

"I thought we were making pretty good time. Those old stones are heavy and the mortar is surprisingly intact."

Bashir seemed to take in the surroundings. "Ah, yes," it said and that wide, wide mouth broke into a grin of wicked sharp teeth. "I don't suppose they build them like this any more."

"They don't. So, what are we going to do about you?"

Bashir slid off the chest and crawled cautiously in my direction. It neared an etched symbol about a foot away from my boot and glared hatefully at it.

"What," it asked, bringing the clawed fingers and thumb of one hand to a chin with bristles like the ends of fence wire, "would you like to do about me?"

"Actually, I really wish you weren't here."

"That makes two of us."

"I'll bet. And these etchings on the floor—they make this place a prison for you, correct?"

It tilted its head. "We wouldn't be having this conversation if they didn't."

"And if I were to just walk over there and grab that chest … I have the feeling that would not go so well for me. Am I right?"

Bashir sprang to its cloven feet, sweeping a leathery palm toward the centre of the room. "Come on in and find out."

"I think not."

The creature edged a little closer and suddenly winced. Looking me up and down, it sniffed the air in a series of rapid inhalations.

"You're not a priest," Bashir said, crinkling its snout-like nose. "You don't smell like priest … and you're too thin."

I chuckled. "No, I'm not a priest."

"Then what are you? And what are you doing here?"

I stubbed out my cigarette on the floor beside me. "Funny. Those are exactly the two questions I had for you."

"Too bad." Bashir's dark lips peeled back into an even broader smile. "I asked first."

"Roger?"

Chester's voice echoed from the Ante-Chamber. He stumbled into the Relic Room, the beam of his flashlight dancing off the walls.

"Over here," I called. "But don't come any closer. I'll come to you."

"A moment, please," I said to Bashir as I rose to my feet, grabbed the lantern and walked the perimeter of the wall to where Chester waited for me.

"Apparently it speaks," Chester said as I drew near.

"In time," I replied, "it might be getting it to shut up that could prove the problem. You brought The Book?"

"In the Ante-Chamber. I thought it wiser. Plus, the light is better in there."

Bashir had made its way across the room and was staring at Chester. Those yellow eyes seemed to look right through him. Bashir sniffed the air.

"Now this one," it said with a guttural purr, "this one smells just like a priest. Am I right?"

Chester looked at me questioningly. I could tell he didn't want to address the thing directly and was hoping that I would do it for him. I sighed and shrugged.

"Only half right, Bashir." I nodded toward the Ante-Chamber and Chester left me alone with the creature. "Our man Chester was a priest, but no longer."

"Lapsed, is he?"

"No. Dedicated. I'm yet to meet a more decent or pious man. He may no longer have vestments, but our man Chester still has character. I'll take that any day."

"And rightly so. Keep him safe then, Roger. Pious men are hard to come by."

"Exactly so. Now, if you'll excuse us for a moment, we're going to see if there's a solution to our mutual problem."

Bashir bowed low. "Good luck. I'll be waiting right here."

In the Ante-Chamber, Chester had redirected one of the halogen lamps toward the card table set against the southern wall. My notes and logbook were pushed to one side and The Book rested where we could read it.

The Book belonged in a museum. The covers were wooden, a pair of thinly-sliced sheets of walnut. The bindings were hammered iron, the velum pages held in place with a trio of ancient bolts. Iron hinges connected the covers to the binding and they opened with an age-old cry of protest.

"I looked back at the oldest entries," Chester began. "I soon realized that was a mistake."

"Why a mistake?" I had a feeling I knew where he was going.

"That other bricked up entry. Factory-made bricks—twentieth century bricks. My guess is that thing has only been down here a hundred years at most."

"Bashir," I said absently as I turned The Book toward me, carefully leafing through the faded handwritten pages, passing decades with each turn.

"I beg your pardon?"

"Bashir. The creature wants us to call it Bashir."

"Though that won't be its real name, you know."

I had come to the last of the pages with writing on them, though there were dozens of blank sheets at the end.

"Yes. Apparently that is not its true and secret name. Hello …" My eyes didn't see it, but the pad of my thumb felt it. One of the remaining blank pages was thicker than the others … twice as thick. "Jesus, Chester. How could we have missed this before?"

Cautiously, for I knew The Book to be over seven hundred years old, I picked at the corner of the double-thick page and succeeded in loosening an edge. My thumbnail managed to turn up a corner. I stopped and turned The Book back to Chester.

"Here," I said. "You have a gentler hand than me. You do it."

Chester gently grasped the turned-up corner and painstakingly separated the two stuck-together sheets. He looked down and smiled.

"Whoever wrote this didn't wait for it to dry."

Sure enough. The revealed sheets held ink from a fountain pen. The right-hand page was legible, the left a smeared, ghostly reflection.

"It's German, Chester. Can you do the honors?"

He was already pulling on his reading glasses. "Ein moment, bitte …"

Two minutes later Chester pulled off his glasses, folded the arms and tucked them in his pocket. "Verbatim, or condensed version?"

"Just the gist, my friend."

"Well. Your chum Bashir has only been down here for seventy-three years. The entry is dated November 16th 1936. It was written by Father Hans Langer."

"That makes sense. He was the priest here when it was bombed in 1942."

"He says that on November 13th, a delegation arrived from Rome. They had with them a Holy *Zauberer*—a Papal Magician. He was told that Rome was unwilling to allow the Relic to fall into Nazi hands so they were taking extraordinary steps to ensure its safety. My God. Extraordinary steps indeed."

"Does he tell us precisely what Bashir is?"

"He calls it both *Dämon* and *Teufel-Laich*—that's Demon and Devil-spawn—but nothing more specific. He doesn't mention the type or degree of creature that Bashir is. Without that information I don't know what we can do."

"I do." I pulled out my cell phone. "Earlier—when you called me at the Guesthaus—were you down here?"

"Yes. I was surprised, too. Excellent cell reception down here—better than down the hill in the village. Who are you calling?"

"The boss. She'll know what to do."

I hit the speed dial and waited. It rang twice before her assistant answered. I rattled off the situation and got to wait some more. Dealing across multiple time zones is always a royal pain in the ass. Finally, my employer came on the line.

"I'm told this is not the phone call I wanted, Roger. I'm told we have an unanticipated squatter."

"That's correct, Ma'am." I cleared my throat. It doesn't matter how many times I speak with her, my boss still intimidates the shit out of me. "Frankly, I'm not sure how to deal with Bashir."

"It has a name, does it? Can you tell me the classification of your demon squatter?"

I edged back to the doorway so I could look at Bashir as I spoke to her. It had returned to the chest. When it saw me, it gave me a little wave with that heavily clawed hand. "I can't. He's intelligent. He's articulate. Actually, he's a little bit charming."

"Charming? Yes, they can be that. By the way, you're referring to it as 'he.' Were you aware of that?"

"No, Ma'am. I was not."

"Don't make that mistake. Don't like it too much. Have no doubt that whatever you have there, it is a monster and will tear you to ribbons if given half a chance."

"Understood, Ma'am."

"Are you looking at it now?"

"I am. Yes, Ma'am."

"Describe it to me."

I did. As I spoke, Bashir must have known what I was doing. It showed me its claws, its fangs, its crown of horns, its cloven feet and its ridged tail, complete with serrated barb. It was the description of the tail that cinched it for my boss.

"Baccu-demon," she said, actually sounding relieved. "We might be able to work with this."

"What do you mean, Ma'am? Is this a nice demon?"

"Good Lord, no. The Baccu are as bad as they get. They do have one redeeming quality, however. They are creatures of their word."

"Trustworthy, are they?"

"Not so much, but if you can get it to promise you something, it will abide by its promise."

"You're sure, Ma'am?"

"Absolutely. Are we done?"

I scratched my head.

"How exactly do you want me to proceed?"

"Oh, for God's sake, Roger. You're there. I'm not. You're a bright boy. Figure it out, but always remember—we need that

Relic and we need it now. You know what's at stake. Do what you must."

I snapped shut the phone and pocketed it.

"Chester?" I called over my shoulder. He was at my elbow in a heartbeat.

"What did she say?"

"She told me what I need to know. Now, here's what I need you to do. Take The Book and get in the Land Rover. Start driving toward Nordlingen and don't stop until I call you."

"Is this what the boss said? I don't like the idea of leaving you—"

I pressed my hand on his back. "Go. Drive. If you don't hear from me by morning assume something has gone terribly wrong and get the boss involved. Otherwise, we'll be having a celebratory breakfast down at the café."

"I don't—"

"Don't think. Just drive."

Chester gathered The Book and left. I stood in the ruins and watched until his taillights passed through the village and were swallowed by the night. I took the time to enjoy a cigarette in the open air before mentally girding myself to do what needed to be done.

When I returned to the Relic Room the demon stood in front of the chest, its hands on its hips. Tilting its head, it raised one of its corrugated brow ridges. That wickedly barbed tail flitted endlessly and silently.

"The other one—the little priest-that-was-but-is-no-more—no longer here?"

"Gone," I said. "I sent him away. We need to have a discussion, you and I. Such discussions are best held, I find, out of earshot of pious men."

Bashir sprang forward, coming to a stop at the etched glyph before me. The speed of the thing stole my breath ... And put to rest any illusions I had about being a match for it physically.

"I am so very eager for conversation. Does this talk have anything to do with that little talkie box you were speaking into earlier?"

"It's called a phone. And yes, it has everything to do with that call."

Bashir rubbed those wiry chin hairs in a remarkably human contemplative gesture. "I take it you are after what's in the box."

"In the chest, yes. We're very interested."

Bashir smiled. "Are you sure you know what's in there?"

"Pretty sure."

"But not absolutely sure. What do you *think* is in the box, Roger?"

"That would be telling. Do you know what's in the box?"

"Of course I know."

"So you've opened it then?"

Bashir looked offended. "Please. Someone like me needn't open a box to know what's in it. Now … what are we going to do?"

I ran my fingers through my hair. "You probably don't know this, being trapped in here as you are, but there is a storm on the horizon. Something big and decisive and world-changing is on the way."

"I have sensed certain … vibrations, of late. What you say makes a certain sense. You think what's in the box is going to save you?"

"It and dozens of others like it, yes. Or at least help. Sides are being chosen. Lines are being drawn. That's what we need to talk about."

"I'm listening."

"I am prepared to make you a deal."

"Ohhhhhh. I'm really listening now. Deals … deals are always good."

"I will release you from this place, but I need two promises from you. I am led to believe that your promises tend to be kept."

"My promises *must* be kept. It's who we are. Our word is literally our bond."

"Then this is easy." I let some of the tension drain from my shoulders. "I need you to promise me that if I release you from your prison you will bring no harm in any way to any human and that in the coming conflict you will pick no side. You'll keep your head down and won't become involved. Do we have a bargain?"

The demon sighed and hung its head.

"What's wrong?" I asked. "This is a perfect solution. Both of us get what we want. What's the problem?"

"Your conditions … I have no issue with the latter. I can happily avoid this coming conflict. It's what I would do anyway. It's the former I cannot accommodate."

"The former? Are you telling me that you are incapable of leaving humanity alone?"

Bashir's tail swirled endlessly, drawing elaborate patterns in the air. "The vast bulk of humanity I can leave alone … just not all of it."

"Care to elaborate for me?"

Bashir turned its yellow eyes toward the ceiling. Once it had gathered its thoughts, the demon met my eyes.

"We are creatures of our word, we Baccu," Bashir began, "and therein, Roger, is our shared dilemma."

"I don't understand."

"How long have I been down here, imprisoned in this place?"

"According to The Book, about seventy-three years."

"Really?" Bashir shrugged. "It feels much longer. When I was originally trapped here, I did a foolish thing. I railed against my captor."

"I would expect nothing less."

Bashir shook its head. "You don't understand. I lost my temper. I didn't rail against the sorcerer—he was only doing his job. It was the priest of this church who bore my wrath. I mean really, what kind of priest allows a sorcerer, even a Papal Sorcerer, to enslave a demon on top of his church's holiest relic? Why, that's blasphemy, isn't it?"

"So you lost your temper? So what?"

"Powerless as I was, I did the only thing I could. I vowed revenge upon the priest."

I shrugged. "Too late for that. Father Langer died when the church above us was bombed."

"I also vowed to murder, most unpleasantly, the issue of his loins."

"Well, that's kind of silly. What issue of his loins? The guy was a priest, after all."

A disappointed look crept across Bashir's features. "You certainly don't know much about priests, do you?"

"I know they aren't supposed to have sex with their flock."

"You don't know a lot about shepherds, either. The point is, I vowed revenge upon the issue of his loins and I must have it. A vow is, after all, a promise and we Baccu follow through on all promises."

"Well, I have no idea if he had children, illegitimate or otherwise."

Bashir nodded. "But I do. I have felt the ebb and flow of his bloodline for three generations. I can smell and feel his issue in the village below. That is why, you see, I cannot promise you to leave *all* humanity alone. An earlier vow takes precedence."

I let out a sigh, running fingers through my hair. I swallowed. My skin crawled as I asked the next question.

"How many people are we talking about? You know, down in the village?"

I could see the gears working behind those yellow eyes. "Nine." Bashir said, and then amended. "Well, nine and a half if you count the little bastard festering in the teenager's womb."

"I'll be right back."

I needed to get out. I fled as far as the foot of the steps leading from the Ante-Chamber before I stopped. Reaching into my jacket pocket, I drew out the cell phone and flipped it open. The boss's number stood waiting on the redial screen. I stared at the display for thirty long seconds before I snapped the phone shut.

I could have called the boss and put it all onto her. I could have shifted the responsibility, but I've never been one to make phone calls simply to cover my ass. Especially when I'd already been told to handle things myself.

I crossed the room. As I neared the hole that led to the Relic Room I reached out and grabbed the sledge hammer I had been swinging earlier in the day. It felt good in my hands, weighty and formidable.

I approached quickly and for a moment thought I saw a flicker of surprise cross the demon's face. I stopped just short of the nearest flagstone etched with those arcane symbols far older than Christianity.

"Do I have your word?" I asked, hoping the frenzy I felt within wasn't creeping into my voice.

"My word?" Bashir eyed the sledge hammer I had raised above my shoulder.

"Your word. You take no sides in the coming conflict and that except for the nine descendants of Father Hans Langer—"

"Nine and a half."

"Whatever—except for his direct descendants in the village below you will bring no grief nor harm to humanity for as long as you exist?"

"Well ..."

"Yes or no? Tell me now."

"You have my promise."

I don't remember initiating the swing of shoulders and the sway of hips that brought the sledge hammer thundering down. I only recall the bone-numbing vibration cascading through my arms as the flagstone shattered into a dozen fractured shards.

Bashir swept past me, eager to get on with its business, but the demon paused long enough to run its fingertips along my cheek.

"A pleasure," Bashir purred as it whispered by me. "I'm good to my word. We shall not meet again."

As I hauled the chains from the tar-coated chest I reminded myself that in all wars there are innocent casualties ... acceptable losses ... sustained for the benefit of the greater good.

I also told myself that the soul-chilling sounds I could hear coming from the village were merely some trick of the wind winding through the ruins above and down the spiral stair.

The village was so far away.

Surely no one's screams could ever have carried that far.

✗

Dave's short fiction has appeared in various anthologies and his SF story, "The Last Repairman," which appeared online at *Daily Science Fiction* has received praise and attention from Hollywood to Karachi. In 2011, Dave's unpublished novel, *The Platinum Ticket*, was one of six short-listed novels from a field of 500 for the inaugural Terry Pratchett Prize. Dave lives in a small town northwest of Toronto with his wife, two kids, three ridiculous chickens and a pond full of feral goldfish. To find out more about Dave visit www.davebeynon.com

SURF'S UP!

by Meg Opperman

"Hey you, kid! You can't park your board here." I glared at the teenaged punk, long-board tucked under his skinny arm as he trudged through the sand toward the water. *Our* water. *Our* beach. There were other beaches further north where they'd accept anyone. This wasn't *those* beaches. Of course the other beaches didn't have the A-frame waves we did, but that was only because *we* blocked every effort of local government to institute measures for erosion control. Totally ruins the waves.

Phil and Steve flanked me as we moved in. A dose of intimidation should have the little beaner running for home. Or at least to the taco shop down the street.

"W-what?" The kid stopped, blinked at us like he'd been in a daze. He swept a hand through long black bangs, feet shifting in the sand.

"You heard me. Move along. We don't like strangers. Especially *your* kind."

His eyes widened. If not for that, I wouldn't have noticed his irises weren't the usual mud brown, but a startling violet. Don't even get me started about Mexicans mixing with the rest of us. Guess that's one way to get a green card.

"This isn't a private beach." His back straightened and his knuckles whitened where they held the board.

Ballsy kid, I'll give him that.

"Yeah, it kind of is. See, my friends and I've been surfing it for more than thirty years. That makes it ours. And the Bayside Buds don't let just anybody have a paddle."

"Still not a private beach. I'm just here to ride my sled in peace." His voice cracked as he said it, but he actually put his back to us and continued toward *our* surf.

Not in this lifetime.

I nodded to Phil and Steve and we hurried around to form a wall between him and the waves. I poked the little hombre center mass.

"Need to leave, *amigo.*"

He rubbed at his chest where I'd struck, his face scrunched in a scowl.

"Whatever. You old carp don't need to get your tighty-whities in a bunch." And he walked around us like we weren't even there.

This meant war.

A longer campaign than we anticipated, I'll admit. Phil managed to trip the kid more than once as he came from the surf and Steve and I repeatedly snowballed him, making the waves break before their time. He wouldn't get a good run if we had anything to say about it. When Frank and Rich showed up, they joined in taunting him and laughing whenever he'd take gas or his takeoff was too slow.

Finally, after several hours and one nasty spinout—hodad—the kid had enough and packed it in. We trailed him to a beat-up minivan and watched him strap his board to the top. Instead of surfing bumper stickers, the van was littered with Camp Pendleton logos. Guess the kid had dreams, not that they'd do him much good here. I smiled. He did an admirable job of ignoring us and if he'd applied for a job at my software company, I'd have been impressed by his *cojones*—see, I can get down with their speech. But this was Bayside Beach and that put things in a different light.

As the kid put pedal to the metal he shot us the bird.

"Kids these days." Phil shook his head. I couldn't agree more.

✗   ✗   ✗   ✗

Imagine my surprise when the kid pulled up in his minivan the next weekend. He climbed out, unstrapped his board like he belonged. Only he didn't.

Frank saw him as soon as I did.

"This is going to take a more direct approach," he muttered. I nodded. After calls in to the guys, we watched as the kid paddled into the waves, not bothering to stand up. Dick-dragging. Might as well body board. Frank grunted, noticing, too.

Within fifteen minutes a couple of Hummers, two Land Rovers and a … Prius—effing Phil just *had* to be different—pulled up. Reinforcements arrived. Let's see how he liked getting fin chopped—Steve excelled at that move—and several of us made it our mission to paddle battle him for the waves.

After a particularly nasty fin chop, the kid got worked hard and when he came up from the surf his face was all scraped up.

"That had to hurt." I rammed my shoulder into him as I passed and he fell on his ass. The guys laughed.

"You know, I can call the cops if you keep harassing me."

We all laughed harder.

"You do that, *hombre*. And while you're at it you should tell the sheriff to arrest the mayor's brother-in-law"—I pointed to Frank, who gave a middle finger salute—"and councilman Andrews"—I indicated Rich.

I swear the kid's lip trembled and those weird eyes blinked back tears, but the little beaner turned back into the surf. What the hell? What was it going to take to convince this kid to move along?

Another hour of harassment did the trick. He practically ran to his van, threw his board in the back—no respect for the Fiberglas—and peeled out. I wonder if he liked all the slurs we sketched on his windows with surf wax? Just something to remember us by.

✗ ✗ ✗ ✗

A couple of months later the kid showed up again. Couldn't believe it. Neither could the guys. We surrounded him before he even unpacked his board.

"Thought you'd learned your lesson." I had a good couple of inches and at least forty pounds on the kid, so I used it to my advantage and leaned into his space.

"I did." He smiled, cocksure, his weird-colored eyes laughing at us. "I'm just here to watch."

We all exchanged confused looks.

"Oh, not you guys. I'm watching them." He pointed down the beach where a large barge floated in the surf, covered in concrete pylons that looked like a bunch of stubby jacks the size of a small car. We hadn't even noticed it rolling in. Oh my God, a wave break. No! We'd blocked the city's every effort. No way was this was happening.

The guys all started yelling, but I noticed a work crew on the shore and rushed over to confront them. Heads. Would. Roll.

As I approached the crew, the guy in charge seemed to realize I was barreling down on him with a whole lot of anger and influence. He moved to meet me, stupid looking tinted goggles taking up half his face, a thick stack of official papers clutched in his fist.

"What the hell are you doing?" I shouted. "You don't have authorization to do this—"

"Actually I do, sir." He flashed his Army Corps of Engineers lanyard in my face. "The lack of erosion protection has been deemed a risk to Camp Pendleton and an ecological hazard to the marine wildlife. This artificial reef we're putting in will help break up the wave erosion and create a marine preserve." He flapped the permits under my nose.

The crew chief's radio squawked. "Ready, sir."

"Make it so, Miguel."

"Wait! Pendleton's south of here! It's not at risk. It will ruin the beach!" By now the other guys and a dozen other locals crowded around, all wanting answers. We watched in horror as the pylons spilled into the water. *Our* water.

"Don't worry, sir. I'm sure there are other beaches that will accept *your* kind." The crew chief smiled, pulled off his goggles.

Violet eyes stared back.

✗

Meg Opperman, a cultural anthropologist by training, has mastered the art of eavesdropping in bars around the globe in search of a story. She's had short stories published in both *EQMM* and *SHMM*, and writes a column (Write Side Up) for the *Washington Independent Review of Books*.

THE NAVAL TREATY

by Sir Arthur Conan Doyle

The July which immediately succeeded my marriage was made memorable by three cases of interest, in which I had the privilege of being associated with Sherlock Holmes and of studying his methods. I find them recorded in my notes under the headings of "The Adventure of the Second Stain," "The Adventure of the Naval Treaty," and "The Adventure of the Tired Captain." The first of these, however, deals with interest of such importance and implicates so many of the first families in the kingdom that for many years it will be impossible to make it public. No case, however, in which Holmes was engaged has ever illustrated the value of his analytical methods so clearly or has impressed those who were associated with him so deeply. I still retain an almost verbatim report of the interview in which he demonstrated the true facts of the case to Monsieur Dubugue of the Paris police, and Fritz von Waldbaum, the well-known specialist of Dantzig, both of whom had wasted their energies upon what proved to be side-issues. The new century will have come, however, before the story can be safely told. Meanwhile I pass on to the second on my list, which promised also at one time to be of national importance, and was marked by several incidents which give it a quite unique character.

During my school-days I had been intimately associated with a lad named Percy Phelps, who was of much the same age as myself, though he was two classes ahead of me. He was a very brilliant boy, and carried away every prize which the school had to offer, finished his exploits by winning a scholarship which sent him on to continue his triumphant career at Cambridge. He was, I remember, extremely well connected, and even when we were all little boys together we knew that his mother's brother was Lord Holdhurst, the great conservative politician. This gaudy relationship did him little good at school. On the contrary, it seemed rather a piquant thing to us to chevy him about the playground and hit him over the shins with a wicket. But it was another thing when he came out into the world. I heard vaguely that his abilities and the influences which he commanded had won him a good position at the Foreign Office, and then he passed completely out of my mind until the following letter recalled his existence:

Briarbrae, Woking.

MY DEAR WATSON–

I have no doubt that you can remember "Tadpole" Phelps, who was in the fifth form when you were in the third. It is possible even that you may have heard that through my uncle's influence I obtained a good appointment at the Foreign Office, and that I was in a situation of trust and honour until a horrible misfortune came suddenly to blast my career.

There is no use writing of the details of that dreadful event. In the event of your acceding to my request it is probably that I shall have to narrate them to you. I have only just recovered from nine weeks of brain-fever, and am still exceedingly weak. Do you think that you could bring your friend Mr Holmes down to see me? I should like to have his opinion of the case, though the authorities assure me that nothing more can be done. Do try to bring him down, and as soon as possible. Every minute seems an hour while I live in this state of horrible suspense. Assure him that if I have not asked his advice sooner it was not because I did not appreciate his talents, but because I have been off my head ever since the blow fell. Now I am clear again, though I dare not think of it too much for fear of a relapse. I am still so weak that I have to write, as you see, by dictating. Do try to bring him.

Your old school-fellow,
PERCY PHELPS

There was something that touched me as I read this letter, something pitiable in the reiterated appeals to bring Holmes. So moved was I that even had it been a difficult matter I should have tried it, but of course I knew well that Holmes loved his art, so that he was ever as ready to bring his aid as his client could be to receive it. My wife agreed with me that not a moment should be lost in laying the matter before him, and so within an hour of breakfast-time I found myself back once more in the old rooms in Baker Street.

Holmes was seated at his side-table clad in his dressing-gown, and working hard over a chemical investigation. A large curved retort was boiling furiously in the bluish flame of a Bunsen burner, and the distilled drops were condensing into a two-litre measure. My friend hardly glanced up as I entered, and I, seeing that his investigation must be of importance, seated myself in an arm-chair and waited. He dipped into this bottle or that, drawing out a few drops of each with his glass pipette, and finally brought a test-tube containing a solution over to the table. In his right hand he held a slip of litmus-paper.

"You come at a crisis, Watson," said he. "If this paper remains blue, all is well. If it turns red, it means a man's life." He dipped it into the test-tube and it flushed at once into a dull, dirty crimson. "Hum! I thought as much!" he cried. "I will be at your service in an instant, Watson. You will find tobacco in the Persian slipper." He turned to his desk and scribbled off several telegrams, which were handed over to the page-boy. Then he threw himself down into the chair opposite, and drew up his knees until his fingers clasped round his long, thin shins.

"A very commonplace little murder," said he. "You've got something better, I fancy. You are the stormy petrel of crime, Watson. What is it?"

I handed him the letter, which he read with the most concentrated attention.

"It does not tell us very much, does it?" he remarked, as he handed it back to me.

"Hardly anything."

"And yet the writing is of interest."

"But the writing is not his own."

"Precisely. It is a woman's."

"A man's surely," I cried.

"No, a woman's, and a woman of rare character. You see, at the commencement of an investigation it is something to know that your client is in close contact with some one who, for good or evil, has an exceptional nature. My interest is already awakened in the case. If you are ready we will start at once for Woking, and see this diplomatist who is in such evil case, and the lady to whom he dictates his letters."

We were fortunate enough to catch an early train at Waterloo, and in a little under an hour we found ourselves among the fir-woods and the heather of Woking. Briarbrae proved to be a large detached house standing in extensive grounds within a few minutes' walk of the station. On sending in our cards we were shown into an elegantly appointed drawing-room, where we were joined in a few minutes by a rather stout man who received us with much hospitality. His age may have been nearer forty than thirty, but his cheeks were so ruddy and his eyes so merry that he still conveyed the impression of a plump and mischievous boy.

"I am so glad that you have come," said he, shaking our hands with effusion. "Percy has been inquiring for you all morning. Ah, poor old chap, he clings to any straw! His father and his mother asked me to see you, for the mere mention of the subject is very painful to them."

"We have had no details yet," observed Holmes. "I perceive that you are not yourself a member of the family."

Our acquaintance looked surprised, and then, glancing down, he began to laugh.

"Of course you saw the J H monogram on my locket," said he. "For a moment I thought you had done something clever. Joseph Harrison is my name, and as Percy is to marry my sister Annie I shall at least be a relation by marriage. You will find my sister in his room, for she has nursed him hand-and-foot this two months back. Perhaps we'd better go in at once, for I know how impatient he is."

The chamber in which we were shown was on the same floor as the drawing-room. It was furnished partly as a sitting and partly as a bedroom, with flowers arranged daintily in every nook and corner. A young man, very pale and worn, was lying upon a sofa near the open window, through which came the rich scent of the garden and the balmy summer air. A woman was sitting beside him, who rose as we entered.

"Shall I leave, Percy?" she asked.

He clutched her hand to detain her. "How are you, Watson?" said he, cordially. "I should never have known you under that moustache, and I dare say you would not be prepared to swear to me. This I presume is your celebrated friend, Mr Sherlock Holmes?"

I introduced him in a few words, and we both sat down. The stout young man had left us, but his sister still remained with her hand in that of the invalid. She was a striking-looking woman, a little short and thick for symmetry, but with a beautiful olive complexion, large, dark, Italian eyes, and a wealth of deep black hair. Her rich tints made the white face of her companion the more worn and haggard by the contrast.

"I won't waste your time," said he, raising himself upon the sofa. "I'll plunge into the matter without further preamble. I was a happy and successful man, Mr Holmes, and on the eve of being married, when a sudden and dreadful misfortune wrecked all my prospects in life.

"I was, as Watson may have told you, in the Foreign Office, and through the influences of my uncle, Lord Holdhurst, I rose rapidly to a responsible position. When my uncle became foreign minister in this administration he gave me several missions of trust, and as I always brought them to a successful conclusion, he came at last to have the utmost confidence in my ability and tact.

"Nearly ten weeks ago—to be more accurate, on the 23d of May—he called me into his private room, and, after complimenting me on the good work which I had done, he informed me that he had a new commission of trust for me to execute.

"'This,' said he, taking a grey roll of paper from his bureau, 'is the original of that secret treaty between England and Italy of which, I regret to say, some rumours have already got into the public press. It is of enormous importance that nothing further should leak out. The French or the Russian embassy would pay an immense sum to learn the contents of these papers. They should not leave my bureau were it not that it is absolutely necessary to have them copied. You have a desk in your office?'

"'Yes, sir.'

"'Then take the treaty and lock it up there. I shall give directions that you may remain behind when the others go, so that you may copy it at your leisure without fear of being overlooked. When you have finished, relock both the original and the draft in the desk, and hand them over to me personally to-morrow morning.'

"I took the papers and—"

"Excuse me an instant," said Holmes. "Were you alone during this conversation?"

"Absolutely."

"In a large room?"

"Thirty feet each way."

"In the centre?"

"Yes, about it."

"And speaking low?"

"My uncle's voice is always remarkably low. I hardly spoke at all."

"Thank you," said Holmes, shutting his eyes; "pray go on."

"I did exactly what he indicated, and waited until the other clerks had departed. One of them in my room, Charles Gorot, had some arrears of work to make up, so I left him there and went out to dine. When I returned he was gone. I was anxious to hurry my work, for I knew that Joseph—the Mr Harrison whom you saw just now—was in town, and that he would travel down to Woking by the eleven-o'clock train, and I wanted if possible to catch it.

"When I came to examine the treaty I saw at once that it was of such importance that my uncle had been guilty of no exaggeration in what he had said. Without going into details, I may say that it defined the position of Great Britain towards the Triple Alliance, and fore-shadowed the policy which this country would pursue in the event of the French fleet gaining a complete ascendancy over that of Italy in the Mediterranean. The questions treated in it were purely naval. At the end were the signatures of the high dignitaries who had signed it. I glanced my eyes over it, and then settled down to my task of copying.

"It was a long document, written in the French language, and containing twenty-six separate articles. I copied as quickly as I could, but at nine o'clock I had only done nine articles, and it seemed hopeless for me to attempt to catch my train. I was feeling drowsy and stupid, partly from my dinner and also from the effects of a long day's work. A cup of coffee would clear my brain. A commissionaire remains all night in a little lodge at the foot of the stairs, and is in the habit of making coffee at his spirit-lamp for any of the officials who may be working overtime. I rang the bell, therefore, to summon him.

"To my surprise, it was a woman who answered the summons, a large, coarse-faced, elderly woman, in an apron. She explained that she was the commissionaire's wife, who did the charing, and I gave her the order for the coffee.

"I wrote two more articles and then, feeling more drowsy than ever, I rose and walked up and down the room to stretch my legs. My coffee had not yet come, and I wondered what the cause of the delay could be. Opening the door, I started down the corridor to find out. There was a straight passage, dimly lighted, which led from the room in which I had been working, and was the only exit from it. It ended in a curving staircase, with the commissionaire's lodge in the passage at the bottom. Half way down this staircase is a small landing, with another passage running into it at right angles. This second one leads by means of a second small stair to a side door, used by servants, and also as a short cut by clerks when coming from Charles Street. Here is a rough chart of the place."

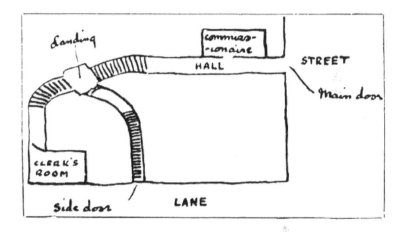

"Thank you. I think that I quite follow you," said Sherlock Holmes.

"It is of the utmost importance that you should notice this point. I went down the stairs and into the hall, where I found the commissionaire fast asleep in his box, with the kettle boiling furiously upon the spirit-lamp. I took off the kettle and blew out the lamp, for the water was spurting over the floor. Then I put out my hand and was about to shake the man, who was still sleeping soundly, when a bell over his head rang loudly, and he woke with a start.

"'Mr Phelps, sir!' said he, looking at me in bewilderment.

"'I came down to see if my coffee was ready.'

"'I was boiling the kettle when I fell asleep, sir.' He looked at me and then up at the still quivering bell with an ever-growing astonishment upon his face.

"'If you was here, sir, then who rang the bell?' he asked.

"'The bell!' I cried. 'What bell is it?'

"'It's the bell of the room you were working in.'

"A cold hand seemed to close round my heart. Someone, then, was in that room where my precious treaty lay upon the table. I ran frantically up the stair and along the passage. There was no one in the corridors, Mr Holmes. There was no one in the room. All was exactly as I left it, save only that the papers which had been committed to my care had been taken from the desk on which they lay. The copy was there, and the original was gone."

Holmes sat up in his chair and rubbed his hands. I could see that the problem was entirely to his heart. "Pray, what did you do then?" he murmured.

"I recognised in an instant that the thief must have come up the stairs from the side door. Of course I must have met him if he had come the other way."

"You were satisfied that he could not have been concealed in the room all the time, or in the corridor which you have just described as dimly lighted?"

"It is absolutely impossible. A rat could not conceal himself either in the room or the corridor. There is no cover at all."

"Thank you. Pray proceed."

"The commissionaire, seeing by my pale face that something was to be feared, had followed me upstairs. Now we both rushed along the corridor and down the steep steps which led to Charles Street. The door at the bottom was closed, but unlocked. We flung it open and rushed out. I can distinctly remember that as we did so there came three chimes from a neighbouring clock. It was quarter to ten."

"That is of enormous importance," said Holmes, making a note upon his shirt-cuff.

"The night was very dark, and a thin, warm rain was falling. There was no one in Charles Street, but a great traffic was going on, as usual, in Whitehall, at the extremity. We rushed along the pavement, bare-headed as we were, and at the far corner we found a policeman standing.

"'A robbery has been committed,' I gasped. 'A document of immense value has been stolen from the Foreign Office. Has anyone passed this way?'

"'I have been standing here for a quarter of an hour, sir,' said he; 'only one person has passed during that time—a woman, tall and elderly, with a Paisley shawl.'

"'Ah, that is only my wife,' cried the commissionaire; 'has no one else passed?'

"'No one.'

"'Then it must be the other way that the thief took,' cried the fellow, tugging at my sleeve.

"But I was not satisfied, and the attempts which he made to draw me away increased my suspicions.

"'Which way did the woman go?' I cried.

"'I don't know, sir. I noticed her pass, but I had no special reason for watching her. She seemed to be in a hurry.'

"'How long ago was it?'

"'Oh, not very many minutes.'

"'Within the last five?'

"'Well, it could not be more than five.'

"'You're only wasting your time, sir, and every minute now is of importance,' cried the commissionaire; 'take my word for it that my old woman has nothing to do with it, and come down to the other end of the street. Well, if you won't, I will.' And with that he rushed off in the other direction.

"But I was after him in an instant and caught him by the sleeve.

"'Where do you live?' said I.

"'No. 16 Ivy Lane, Brixton,' he answered. 'But don't let yourself be drawn away upon a false scent, Mr Phelps. Come to the other end of the street and let us see if we can hear of anything.'

"Nothing was to be lost by following his advice. With the policeman we both hurried down, but only to find the street full of traffic, many people coming and going, but all only too eager to get to a place of safety upon so wet a night. There was no lounger who could tell us who had passed.

"Then we returned to the office, and searched the stairs and the passage without result. The corridor which led to the room was laid down with a kind of creamy linoleum which shows an impression very easily. We examined it very carefully, but found no outline of any footmark."

"Had it been raining all evening?"

"Since about seven."

"How is it, then, that the woman who came into the room about nine left no traces with her muddy boots?"

"I am glad you raised the point. It occurred to me at the time. The charwomen are in the habit of taking off their boots at the commissionaire's office, and putting on list slippers."

"That is very clear. There were no marks, then, though the night was a wet one? The chain of events is certainly one of extraordinary interest. What did you do next?"

"We examined the room also. There is no possibility of a secret door, and the windows are quite thirty feet from the ground. Both of them were fastened on the inside. The carpet prevents any possibility of a trap-door, and the ceiling is of the ordinary whitewashed kind. I will pledge my life that whoever stole my papers could only have come through the door."

"How about the fireplace?"

"They use none. There is a stove. The bell-rope hangs from the wire just to the right of my desk. Whoever rang it must have come right up to the desk to do it. But why should any criminal wish to ring the bell? It is a most insoluble mystery."

"Certainly the incident was unusual. What were your next steps? You examined the room, I presume, to see if the intruder had left any traces—any cigar-end or dropped glove or hairpin or other trifle?"

"There was nothing of the sort."

"No smell?"

"Well, we never thought of that."

"Ah, a scent of tobacco would have been worth a great deal to us in such an investigation."

"I never smoke myself, so I think I should have observed it if there had been any smell of tobacco. There was absolutely no clue of any kind. The only tangible fact was that the commissionaire's wife—Mrs Tangey was the name—had hurried out of the place. He could give no explanation save that it was about the time when the woman always went home. The policeman and I agreed that our best plan would be to seize the woman before she could get rid of the papers, presuming that she had them.

"The alarm had reached Scotland Yard by this time, and Mr Forbes, the detective, came round at once and took up the case with a great deal of energy. We hired a hansom, and in half an hour we were at the address which had been given to us. A young woman opened the door, who proved to be Mrs Tangey's eldest daughter. Her mother had not come back yet, and we were shown into the front room to wait.

"About ten minutes later a knock came at the door, and here we made the one serious mistake for which I blame myself. Instead of opening the door ourselves, we allowed the girl to do so. We heard her say, 'Mother, there are two men in the house waiting to see you,' and an instant afterwards we heard the patter of feet rushing down the passage. Forbes flung open the door, and we both ran into the back room or kitchen, but the woman had got there before us. She stared at us with defiant eyes, and then, suddenly recognising me, an expression of absolute astonishment came over her face.

"'Why, if it isn't Mr Phelps, of the office!' she cried.

"'Come, come, who did you think we were when you ran away from us?' asked my companion.

"'I thought you were the brokers,' said she, 'we have had some trouble with a tradesman.'

"'That's not quite good enough,' answered Forbes. 'We have reason to believe that you have taken a paper of importance from the Foreign Office, and that you ran in here to dispose of it. You must come back with us to Scotland Yard to be searched.'

"It was in vain that she protested and resisted. A four-wheeler was brought, and we all three drove back in it. We had first made an examination of the kitchen, and especially of the kitchen fire, to see whether she might have made away with the papers during the instant that she was alone. There were no signs, however, of any ashes or scraps. When we reached Scotland Yard she was handed over at once to the female searcher. I waited in an agony of suspense until she came back with her report. There were no signs of the papers.

"Then for the first time the horror of my situation came in its full force. Hitherto I had been acting, and action had numbed thought. I had been so confident of regaining the treaty at once that I had not dared to think of what would be the consequence if I failed to do so. But now there was nothing more to be done, and I had leisure to realise my position. It was horrible. Watson there would tell you that I was a nervous, sensitive boy at school. It is my nature. I thought of my uncle and of his colleagues in the Cabinet, of the shame which I had brought upon him, upon myself, upon everyone connected with me. What though I was the victim of an extraordinary accident? No allowance is made for accidents where diplomatic interests are at stake. I was ruined, shamefully, hopelessly ruined. I don't know what I did. I fancy I must have made a scene. I have a dim recollection of a group of officials who crowded round me, endeavouring to soothe me. One of them drove down with me to Waterloo, and saw me into the Woking train. I believe that he would have come all the way had it not been that Dr Ferrier, who lives near me, was going down by that very train. The doctor most kindly took charge of me, and it was well he did so, for I had a fit in the station, and before we reached home I was practically a raving maniac.

"You can imagine the state of things here when they were roused from their beds by the doctor's ringing and found me in this condition. Poor Annie here and my mother were broken-hearted. Dr Ferrier had just heard enough from the detective at the station to be able to give an idea of what had happened, and his story did not mend matters. It was evident to all that I was in for a long illness, so Joseph was bundled out of this cheery bedroom, and it was turned into a sick-room for me. Here I have lain, Mr Holmes, for over nine weeks, unconscious, and raving with brain-fever. If it had not been for Miss Harrison here and for the doctor's care I should not be speaking to you now. She has nursed me by day and a hired nurse has looked after me by night, for in my mad fits I was capable of anything. Slowly my reason has cleared, but it is only during the last three days that my memory has quite returned. Sometimes I wish that it never had. The first thing that I did was to wire to Mr Forbes, who had the case in hand. He came out, and as-sures me that, though everything has been done, no trace of a clue has been discovered. The commissionaire and his wife have been examined in every way without any light being thrown upon the matter. The suspicions of the police then rested upon young Gorot, who, as you may remember, stayed over-time in the office that night. His remaining behind and his French name were really the only two points which could suggest suspicion; but, as a matter of fact, I did not begin work until he had gone, and his people are of Huguenot extraction, but as English in sympathy and tradition as you and I are. Nothing was found to implicate him in any way, and there the matter dropped. I turn to you, Mr Holmes, as absolutely my last hope. If you fail me, then my honour as well as my position are forever forfeited."

The invalid sank back upon his cushions, tired out by this long recital, while his nurse poured him out a glass of some stimulating medicine. Holmes sat silently, with his head thrown back and his eyes closed, in an attitude which might seem listless to a stranger, but which I knew betokened the most intense self-absorption.

"Your statement has been so explicit," said he at last, "that you have really left me very few questions to ask. There is one of the very utmost importance, however. Did you tell anyone that you had this special task to perform?"

"No one."

"Not Miss Harrison here, for example?"

"No. I had not been back to Woking between getting the order and executing the commission."

"And none of your people had by chance been to see you?"

"None."

"Did any of them know their way about in the office?"

"Oh, yes, all of them had been shown over it."

"Still, of course, if you said nothing to anyone about the treaty these inquiries are irrelevant."

"I said nothing."

"Do you know anything of the commissionaire?"

"Nothing except that he is an old soldier."

"What regiment?"

"Oh, I have heard—Coldstream Guards."

"Thank you. I have no doubt I can get details from Forbes. The authorities are excellent at amassing facts, though they do not always use them to advantage. What a lovely thing a rose is!"

He walked past the couch to the open window, and held up the drooping stalk of a moss-rose, looking down at the dainty blend of crimson and green. It was a new phase of his character to me, for I had never before seen him show any keen interest in natural objects.

"There is nothing in which deduction is so necessary as in religion," said he, leaning with his back against the shutters. "It can be built up as an exact science by the reasoner. Our highest assurance of the goodness of Providence seems to me to rest in the flowers. All other things, our powers, our desires, our food, are all really necessary for our existence in the first instance. But this rose is an extra. Its smell and its colour are an embellishment of life, not a condition of it. It is only goodness which gives extras, and so I say again that we have much to hope from the flowers."

Percy Phelps and his nurse looked at Holmes during this demonstration with surprise and a good deal of disappointment written upon their faces. He had fallen into a reverie, with the moss-rose between his fingers. It had lasted some minutes before the young lady broke in upon it.

"Do you see any prospect of solving this mystery, Mr Holmes?" she asked, with a touch of asperity in her voice.

"Oh, the mystery!" he answered, coming back with a start to the realities of life. "Well, it would be absurd to deny that the case is a very abstruse and complicated one, but I can promise you that I will look into the matter and let you know any points which may strike me."

"Do you see any clue?"

"You have furnished me with seven, but, of course, I must test them before I can pronounce upon their value."

"You suspect someone?"

"I suspect myself."

"What!"

"Of coming to conclusions too rapidly."

"Then go to London and test your conclusions."

"Your advice is very excellent, Miss Harrison," said Holmes, rising. "I think, Watson, we cannot do better. Do not allow yourself to indulge in false hopes, Mr Phelps. The affair is a very tangled one."

"I shall be in a fever until I see you again," cried the diplomatist.

"Well, I'll come out by the same train to-morrow, though it's more than likely that my report will be a negative one."

"God bless you for promising to come," cried our client. "It gives me fresh life to know that something is being done. By the way, I have had a letter from Lord Holdhurst."

"Ha! What did he say?"

"He was cold, but not harsh. I dare say my severe illness prevented him from being that. He repeated that the matter was of the utmost importance, and added that no steps would be taken about my future—by which he means, of course, my dismissal—until my health was restored and I had an opportunity of repairing my misfortune."

"Well, that was reasonable and considerate," said Holmes. "Come, Watson, for we have a good day's work before us in town."

Mr Joseph Harrison drove us down to the station, and we were soon whirling up in a Portsmouth train. Holmes was sunk in profound thought, and hardly opened his mouth until we had passed Clapham Junction.

"It's a very cheery thing to come into London by any of these lines which run high, and allow you to look down upon the houses like this."

I thought he was joking, for the view was sordid enough, but he soon explained himself.

"Look at those big, isolated clumps of buildings rising up above the slates, like brick islands in a lead-coloured sea."

"The board-schools."

"Light-houses, my boy! Beacons of the future! Capsules with hundreds of bright little seeds in each, out of which will spring the wise, better England of the future. I suppose that man Phelps does not drink?"

"I should not think so."

"Nor should I, but we are bound to take every possibility into account. The poor devil has certainly got himself into very deep water, and it's a question whether we shall ever be able to get him ashore. What did you think of Miss Harrison?"

"A girl of strong character."

"Yes, but she is a good sort, or I am mistaken. She and her brother are the only children of an iron-master somewhere up Northumberland way. He got engaged to her when travelling last winter, and she came down to be introduced to his people, with her brother as escort. Then came the smash, and she stayed on to nurse her lover, while brother Joseph, finding himself pretty snug, stayed on too. I've been making a few independent inquiries, you see. But to-day must be a day of inquiries."

"My practice—" I began.

"Oh, if you find your own cases more interesting than mine—" said Holmes, with some asperity.

"I was going to say that my practice could get along very well for a day or two, since it is the slackest time in the year."

"Excellent," said he, recovering his good-humour. "Then we'll look into this matter together. I think that we should begin by seeing Forbes. He can probably tell us all the details we want until we know from what side the case is to be approached."

"You said you had a clue?"

"Well, we have several, but we can only test their value by further inquiry. The most difficult crime to track is the one which is purposeless. Now this is not purposeless. Who is it who profits by it? There is the French ambassador, there is the Russian, there is who-ever might sell it to either of these, and there is Lord Holdhurst."

"Lord Holdhurst!"

"Well, it is just conceivable that a statesman might find himself in a position where he was not sorry to have such a document accidentally destroyed."

"Not a statesman with the honourable record of Lord Holdhurst?"

"It is a possibility and we cannot afford to disregard it. We shall see the noble lord to-day and find out if he can tell us anything. Meanwhile I have already set inquiries on foot."

"Already?"

"Yes, I sent wires from Woking station to every evening paper in London. This advertisement will appear in each of them."

He handed over a sheet torn from a note-book. On it was scribbled in pencil: "£10 reward. The number of the cab which dropped a fare at or about the door of the Foreign Office in Charles Street at quarter to ten in the evening of May 23d. Apply 221 B, Baker Street."

"You are confident that the thief came in a cab?"

"If not, there is no harm done. But if Mr Phelps is correct in stating that there is no hiding-place either in the room or the corridors, then the person must have come from outside. If he came from outside on so wet a night, and yet left no trace of damp upon the linoleum, which was examined within a few minutes of his passing, then it is exceedingly probable that he came in a cab. Yes, I think that we may safely deduce a cab."

"It sounds plausible."

"That is one of the clues of which I spoke. It may lead us to something. And then, of course, there is the bell—which is the most distinctive feature of the case. Why should the bell ring? Was it the thief who did it out of bravado? Or was it someone who was with the thief who did it in order to prevent the crime? Or was it an accident? Or was it—?" He sank back into the state of intense and silent thought from which he had emerged; but it seemed to me, accustomed as I was to his every mood, that some new possibility had dawned suddenly upon him.

It was twenty past three when we reached our terminus, and after a hasty luncheon at the buffet we pushed on at once to Scotland Yard. Holmes had already wired to Forbes, and we found him waiting to receive us—a small, foxy man with a sharp but by no means amiable expression. He was decidedly frigid in his manner to us, especially when he heard the errand upon which we had come.

"I've heard of your methods before now, Mr Holmes," said he, tartly. "You are ready enough to use all the information that the police can lay at your disposal, and then you try to finish the case yourself and bring discredit on them."

"On the contrary," said Holmes, "out of my last fifty-three cases my name has only appeared in four, and the police have had all the credit in forty-nine. I don't blame you for not knowing this, for you are young and inexperienced, but if you wish to get on in your new duties you will work with me and not against me."

"I'd be very glad of a hint or two," said the detective, changing his manner. "I've certainly had no credit from the case so far."

"What steps have you taken?"

"Tangey, the commissionaire, has been shadowed. He left the Guards with a good character and we can find nothing against him. His wife is a bad lot, though. I fancy she knows more about this than appears."

"Have you shadowed her?"

"We have set one of our women on to her. Mrs Tangey drinks, and our woman has been with her twice when she was well on, but she could get nothing out of her."

"I understand that they have had brokers in the house?"

"Yes, but they were paid off."

"Where did the money come from?"

"That was all right. His pension was due. They have not shown any sign of being in funds."

"What explanation did she give of having answered the bell when Mr Phelps rang for the coffee?"

"She said that her husband was very tired and she wished to relieve him."

"Well, certainly that would agree with his being found a little later asleep in his chair. There is nothing against them then but the woman's character. Did you ask her why she hurried away that night? Her haste attracted the attention of the police constable."

"She was later than usual and wanted to get home."

"Did you point out to her that you and Mr Phelps, who started at least twenty minutes after her, got home before her?"

"She explains that by the difference between a 'bus and a hansom."

"Did she make it clear why, on reaching her house, she ran into the back kitchen?"

"Because she had the money there with which to pay off the brokers."

"She has at least an answer for everything. Did you ask her whether in leaving she met anyone or saw any one loitering about Charles Street?"

"She saw no one but the constable."

"Well, you seem to have cross-examined her pretty thoroughly. What else have you done?"

"The clerk Gorot has been shadowed all these nine weeks, but without result. We can show nothing against him."

"Anything else?"

"Well, we have nothing else to go upon—no evidence of any kind."

"Have you formed a theory about how that bell rang?"

"Well, I must confess that it beats me. It was a cool hand, whoever it was, to go and give the alarm like that."

"Yes, it was a queer thing to do. Many thanks to you for what you have told me. If I can put the man into your hands you shall hear from me. Come along, Watson."

"Where are we going to now?" I asked as we left the office.

"We are now going to interview Lord Holdhurst, the cabinet minister and future premier of England."

We were fortunate in finding that Lord Holdhurst was still in his chambers in Downing Street, and on Holmes sending in his card we were instantly shown up. The statesman received us with that old-fashioned courtesy for which he is remarkable, and seated us on the two luxuriant lounges on either side of the fireplace. Standing on the rug between us, with his slight, tall figure, his sharp features, thoughtful face, and curling hair prematurely tinged with grey, he seemed to represent that not to common type, a nobleman who is in truth noble.

"You name is very familiar to me, Mr Holmes," said he, smiling. "And, of course, I cannot pretend to be ignorant of the object of your visit. There has only been one occurrence in these offices which could call for your attention. In whose interest are you acting, may I ask?"

"In that of Mr Percy Phelps," answered Holmes.

"Ah, my unfortunate nephew! You can understand that our kinship makes it the more impossible for me to screen him in any way. I fear that the incident must have a very prejudicial effect upon his career."

"But if the document is found?"

"Ah, that, of course, would be different."

"I had one or two questions which I wished to ask you, Lord Holdhurst."

"I shall be happy to give you any information in my power."

"Was it in this room that you gave your instructions as to the copying of the document?"

"It was."

"Then you could hardly have been overheard?"

"It is out of the question."

"Did you ever mention to anyone that it was your intention to give any one the treaty to be copied?"

"Never."

"You are certain of that?"

"Absolutely."

"Well, since you never said so, and Mr Phelps never said so, and nobody else knew anything of the matter, then the thief's presence in the room was purely accidental. He saw his chance and he took it."

The statesman smiled. "You take me out of my province there," said he.

Holmes considered for a moment. "There is another very important point which I wish to discuss with you," said he. "You feared, as I understand, that very grave results might follow from the details of this treaty becoming known."

A shadow passed over the expressive face of the statesman. "Very grave results indeed."

"And have they occurred?"

"Not yet."

"If the treaty had reached, let us say, the French or Russian Foreign Office, you would expect to hear of it?"

"I should," said Lord Holdhurst, with a wry face.

"Since nearly ten weeks have elapsed, then, and nothing has been heard, it is not unfair to suppose that for some reason the treaty has not reached them."

Lord Holdhurst shrugged his shoulders.

"We can hardly suppose, Mr Holmes, that the thief took the treaty in order to frame it and hang it up."

"Perhaps he is waiting for a better price."

"If he waits a little longer he will get no price at all. The treaty will cease to be secret in a few months."

"That is most important," said Holmes. "Of course, it is a possible supposition that the thief has had a sudden illness—"

"An attack of brain-fever, for example?" asked the statesman, flashing a swift glance at him.

"I did not say so," said Holmes, imperturbably. "And now, Lord Holdhurst, we have already taken up too much of your valuable time, and we shall wish you good-day."

"Every success to your investigation, be the criminal who it may," answered the nobleman, as he bowed us out the door.

"He's a fine fellow," said Holmes, as we came out into White-hall. "But he has a struggle to keep up his position. He is far from rich and has many calls. You noticed, of course, that his boots had been resoled. Now, Watson, I won't detain you from your legitimate work any longer. I shall do nothing more to-day, unless I have an answer to my cab advertisement. But I should be extremely obliged to you if you would come down with me to Woking to-morrow, by the same train which we took yesterday."

I met him accordingly next morning and we travelled down to Woking together. He had had no answer to his advertisement, he said, and no fresh light had been thrown upon the case. He had, when he so willed it, the utter immobility of countenance of a red Indian, and I could not gather from his appearance whether he was satisfied or not with the position of the case. His conversation, I remember, was about the Bertillon system of measurements, and he expressed his enthusiastic admiration of the French savant.

We found our client still under the charge of his devoted nurse, but looking considerably better than before. He rose from the sofa and greeted us without difficulty when we entered.

"Any news?" he asked, eagerly.

"My report, as I expected, is a negative one," said Holmes. "I have seen Forbes, and I have seen your uncle, and I have set one or two trains of inquiry upon foot which may lead to something."

"You have not lost heart, then?"

"By no means."

"God bless you for saying that!" cried Miss Harrison. "If we keep our courage and our patience the truth must come out."

"We have more to tell you than you have for us," said Phelps, reseating himself upon the couch.

"I hoped you might have something."

"Yes, we have had an adventure during the night, and one which might have proved to be a serious one." His expression grew very grave as he spoke, and a look of something akin to fear sprang up in his eyes. "Do you know," said he, "that I begin to believe that I am the unconscious centre of some monstrous conspiracy, and that my life is aimed at as well as my honour?"

"Ah!" cried Holmes.

"It sounds incredible, for I have not, as far as I know, an enemy in the world. Yet from last night's experience I can come to no other conclusion."

"Pray let me hear it."

"You must know that last night was the very first night that I have ever slept without a nurse in the room. I was so much better that I thought I could dispense with one. I had a night-light burning, however. Well, about two in the morning I had sunk into a light sleep when I was suddenly aroused by a slight noise. It was like the sound which a mouse makes when it is gnawing a plank, and I lay listening to it for some time under the impression that it must come from that cause. Then it grew louder, and suddenly there came from the window a sharp metallic snick. I sat up in amazement. There could be no doubt what the sounds were now. The first ones had been caused by someone forcing an instrument through the slit between the sashes, and the second by the catch being pressed back.

"There was a pause then for about ten minutes, as if the person were waiting to see whether the noise had awakened me. Then I heard a gentle creaking as the window was very slowly opened. I could stand it no longer, for my nerves are not what they used to be. I sprang out of bed and flung open the shutters. A man was crouching at the window. I could see little of him, for he was gone like a flash. He was wrapped in some sort of cloak which came across the lower part of his face. One thing only I am sure of, and that is that he had some weapon in his hand. It looked to me like a long knife. I distinctly saw the gleam of it as he turned to run."

"This is most interesting," said Holmes. "Pray what did you do then?"

"I should have followed him through the open window if I had been stronger. As it was, I rang the bell and roused the house. It took me some little time, for the bell rings in the kitchen and the servants all sleep upstairs. I shouted, however, and that brought Joseph down, and he roused the others. Joseph and the groom found marks on the bed outside the window, but the weather has been so dry lately that they found it hopeless to follow the trail across the grass. There's a place, however, on the wooden fence which skirts the road which shows signs, they tell me, as if someone had got over, and had snapped the top of the rail in doing so. I have said nothing to the local police yet, for I thought I had best have your opinion first."

This tale of our client's appeared to have an extraordinary effect upon Sherlock Holmes. He rose from his chair and paced about the room in uncontrollable excitement.

"Misfortunes never come single," said Phelps, smiling, though it was evident that his adventure had somewhat shaken him.

"You have certainly had your share," said Holmes. "Do you think you could walk round the house with me?"

"Oh, yes, I should like a little sunshine. Joseph will come, too."

"And I also," said Miss Harrison.

"I am afraid not," said Holmes, shaking his head. "I think I must ask you to remain sitting exactly where you are."

The young lady resumed her seat with an air of displeasure. Her brother, however, had joined us and we set off all four together. We passed round the lawn to the outside of the young diplomatist's window. There were, as he had said, marks upon the bed, but they were hopelessly blurred and vague. Holmes stopped over them for an instant, and then rose shrugging his shoulders.

"I don't think anyone could make much of this," said he. "Let us go round the house and see why this particular room was chosen by the burglar. I should have thought those larger windows of the drawing-room and dining-room would have had more attractions for him."

"They are more visible from the road," suggested Mr Joseph Harrison.

"Ah, yes, of course. There is a door here which he might have attempted. What is it for?"

"It is the side entrance for trades-people. Of course it is locked at night."

"Have you ever had an alarm like this before?"

"Never," said our client.

"Do you keep plate in the house, or anything to attract burglars?"

"Nothing of value."

Holmes strolled round the house with his hands in his pockets and a negligent air which was unusual with him.

"By the way," said he to Joseph Harrison, "you found some place, I understand, where the fellow scaled the fence. Let us have a look at that!"

The plump young man led us to a spot where the top of one of the wooden rails had been cracked. A small fragment of the wood was hanging down. Holmes pulled it off and examined it critically.

"Do you think that was done last night? It looks rather old, does it not?"

"Well, possibly so."

"There are no marks of any one jumping down upon the other side. No, I fancy we shall get no help here. Let us go back to the bedroom and talk the matter over."

Percy Phelps was walking very slowly, leaning upon the arm of his future brother-in-law. Holmes walked swiftly across the lawn, and we were at the open window of the bedroom long before the others came up.

"Miss Harrison," said Holmes, speaking with the utmost intensity of manner, "you must stay where you are all day. Let nothing prevent you from staying where you are all day. It is of the utmost importance."

"Certainly, if you wish it, Mr Holmes," said the girl in astonishment.

"When you go to bed lock the door of this room on the outside and keep the key. Promise to do this."

"But Percy?"

"He will come to London with us."

"And am I to remain here?"

"It is for his sake. You can serve him. Quick! Promise!"

She gave a quick nod of assent just as the other two came up.

"Why do you sit moping there, Annie?" cried her brother. "Come out into the sunshine!"

"No, thank you, Joseph. I have a slight headache and this room is deliciously cool and soothing."

"What do you propose now, Mr Holmes?" asked our client.

"Well, in investigating this minor affair we must not lose sight of our main inquiry. It would be a very great help to me if you would come up to London with us."

"At once?"

"Well, as soon as you conveniently can. Say in an hour."

"I feel quite strong enough, if I can really be of any help."

"The greatest possible."

"Perhaps you would like me to stay there to-night?"

"I was just going to propose it."

"Then, if my friend of the night comes to revisit me, he will find the bird flown. We are all in your hands, Mr Holmes, and you must tell us exactly what you would like done. Perhaps you would prefer that Joseph came with us so as to look after me?"

"Oh, no; my friend Watson is a medical man, you know, and he'll look after you. We'll have our lunch here, if you will permit us, and then we shall all three set off for town together."

It was arranged as he suggested, though Miss Harrison excused herself from leaving the bedroom, in accordance with Holmes's suggestion. What the object of my friend's manoeuvres was I could not conceive, unless it were to keep the lady away from Phelps, who, rejoiced by his returning health and by the prospect of action, lunched with us in the dining-room. Holmes had a still more startling surprise for us, however, for, after accompanying us down to the station and seeing us into our carriage, he calmly announced that he had no intention of leaving Woking.

"There are one or two small points which I should desire to clear up before I go," said he. "Your absence, Mr Phelps, will in some ways rather assist me. Watson, when you reach London you would oblige me by driving at once to Baker Street with our friend here, and remaining with him until I see you again. It is fortunate that you are old school-fellows, as you must have much to talk over. Mr Phelps can have the spare bedroom to-night, and I will be with you in time for breakfast, for there is a train which will take me into Waterloo at eight."

"But how about our investigation in London?" asked Phelps, ruefully.

"We can do that to-morrow. I think that just at present I can be of more immediate use here."

"You might tell them at Briarbrae that I hope to be back to-morrow night," cried Phelps, as we began to move from the platform.

"I hardly expect to go back to Briarbrae," answered Holmes, and waved his hand to us cheerily as we shot out from the station.

Phelps and I talked it over on our journey, but neither of us could devise a satisfactory reason for this new development.

"I suppose he wants to find out some clues as to the burglary last night, if a burglar it was. For myself, I don't believe it was an ordinary thief."

"What is your own idea, then?"

"Upon my word, you may put it down to my weak nerves or not, but I believe there is some deep political intrigue going on around me, and that for some reason that passes my understanding my life is aimed at by the conspirators. It sounds high-flown and absurd, but consider the facts! Why should a thief try to break in at a bedroom window, where there could be no hope of any plunder, and why should he come with a long knife in his hand?"

"You are sure it was not a house-breaker's jimmy?"

"Oh, no, it was a knife. I saw the flash of the blade quite distinctly."

"But why on earth should you be pursued with such animosity?"

"Ah, that is the question."

"Well, if Holmes takes the same view, that would account for his action, would it not? Presuming that your theory is correct, if he can lay his hands upon the man who threatened you last night he will have gone a long way towards finding who took the naval treaty. It is absurd to suppose that you have two enemies, one of whom robs you, while the other threatens your life."

"But Holmes said that he was not going to Briarbrae."

"I have known him for some time," said I, "but I never knew him do anything yet without a very good reason," and with that our conversation drifted off on to other topics.

But it was a weary day for me. Phelps was still weak after his long illness, and his misfortune made him querulous and nervous. In vain I endeavoured to interest him in Afghanistan, in India, in social questions, in anything which might take his mind out of the groove. He would always come back to his lost treaty, wondering, guessing, speculating, as to what Holmes was doing, what steps Lord Holdhurst was taking, what news we should have in the morning. As the evening wore on his excitement became quite painful.

"You have implicit faith in Holmes?" he asked.

"I have seen him do some remarkable things."

"But he never brought light into anything quite so dark as this?"

"Oh, yes; I have known him solve questions which presented fewer clues than yours."

"But not where such large interests are at stake?"

"I don't know that. To my certain knowledge he has acted on behalf of three of the reigning houses of Europe in very vital matters."

"But you know him well, Watson. He is such an inscrutable fellow that I never quite know what to make of him. Do you think he is hopeful? Do you think he expects to make a success of it?"

"He has said nothing."

"That is a bad sign."

"On the contrary, I have noticed that when he is off the trail he generally says so. It is when he is on a scent and is not quite absolutely sure yet that it is the right one that he is most taciturn. Now, my dear fellow, we can't help matters by making ourselves nervous about them, so let me implore you to go to bed and so be fresh for whatever may await us to-morrow."

I was able at last to persuade my companion to take my advice, though I knew from his excited manner that there was not much hope of sleep for him. Indeed, his mood was infectious, for I lay tossing half the night myself, brooding over this strange problem, and inventing a hundred theories, each of which was more impossible than the last. Why had Holmes remained at Woking? Why had he asked Miss Harrison to remain in the sick-room all day? Why had he been so careful not to inform the people at Briarbrae that he intended to remain near them? I cudgelled my brains until I fell asleep in the endeavour to find some explanation which would cover all these facts.

It was seven o'clock when I awoke, and I set off at once for Phelps's room, to find him haggard and spent after a sleepless night. His first question was whether Holmes had arrived yet.

"He'll be here when he promised," said I, "and not an instant sooner or later."

And my words were true, for shortly after eight a hansom dashed up to the door and our friend got out of it. Standing in the window we saw that his left hand was swathed in a bandage and that his face was very grim and pale. He entered the house, but it was some little time before he came upstairs.

"He looks like a beaten man," cried Phelps.

I was forced to confess that he was right. "After all," said I, "the clue of the matter lies probably here in town."

Phelps gave a groan.

"I don't know how it is," said he, "but I had hoped for so much from his return. But surely his hand was not tied up like that yesterday. What can be the matter?"

"You are not wounded, Holmes?" I asked, as my friend entered the room.

"Tut, it is only a scratch through my own clumsiness," he answered, nodding his good-mornings to us. "This case of yours, Mr Phelps, is certainly one of the darkest which I have ever investigated."

"I feared that you would find it beyond you."

"It has been a most remarkable experience."

"That bandage tells of adventures," said I. "Won't you tell us what has happened?"

"After breakfast, my dear Watson. Remember that I have breathed thirty miles of Surrey air this morning. I suppose that there has been no answer from my cabman advertisement? Well, well, we cannot expect to score every time."

The table was all laid, and just as I was about to ring Mrs Hudson entered with the tea and coffee. A few minutes later she brought in three covers, and we all drew up to the table, Holmes ravenous, I curious, and Phelps in the gloomiest state of depression.

"Mrs Hudson has risen to the occasion," said Holmes, uncovering a dish of curried chicken. "Her cuisine is a little limited, but she has as good an idea of breakfast as a Scotch-woman. What have you here, Watson?"

"Ham and eggs," I answered.

"Good! What are you going to take, Mr Phelps—curried fowl or eggs, or will you help yourself?"

"Thank you. I can eat nothing," said Phelps.

"Oh, come! Try the dish before you."

"Thank you, I would really rather not."

"Well, then," said Holmes, with a mischievous twinkle, "I suppose that you have no objection to helping me?"

Phelps raised the cover, and as he did so he uttered a scream, and sat there staring with a face as white as the plate upon which he looked. Across the centre of it was lying a little cylinder of blue-grey paper. He caught it up, devoured it with his eyes, and then danced madly about the room, pressing it to his bosom and shrieking out in his delight. Then he fell back into an arm-chair so limp and exhausted with his own emotions that we had to pour brandy down his throat to keep him from fainting.

"There! There!" said Holmes soothingly, patting him upon the shoulder. "It was too bad to spring it on you like this, but Watson here will tell you that I never can resist a touch of the dramatic."

Phelps seized his hand and kissed it. "God bless you!" he cried. "You have saved my honour."

"Well, my own was at stake, you know," said Holmes. "I assure you it is just as hateful to me to fail in a case as it can be to you to blunder over a commission."

Phelps thrust away the precious document into the innermost pocket of his coat.

"I have not the heart to interrupt your breakfast any further, and yet I am dying to know how you got it and where it was."

Sherlock Holmes swallowed a cup of coffee, and turned his attention to the ham and eggs. Then he rose, lit his pipe, and settled himself down into his chair.

"I'll tell you what I did first, and how I came to do it afterwards," said he. "After leaving you at the station I went for a charming walk through some admirable Surrey scenery to a pretty little village called Ripley, where I had my tea at an inn, and took the precaution of filling my flask and of putting a paper of sandwiches in my pocket. There I remained until evening, when I set off for Woking again, and found myself in the high-road outside Briarbrae just after sunset.

"Well, I waited until the road was clear—it is never a very frequented one at any time, I fancy—and then I clambered over the fence into the grounds."

"Surely the gate was open!" ejaculated Phelps.

"Yes, but I have a peculiar taste in these matters. I chose the place where the three fir-trees stand, and behind their screen I got over without the least chance of any one in the house being able to see me. I crouched down among the bushes on the other side, and crawled from one to the other—witness the disreputable state of my trouser knees—until I had reached the clump of rhododendrons just opposite to your bedroom window. There I squatted down and awaited developments.

"The blind was not down in your room, and I could see Miss Harrison sitting there reading by the table. It was quarter-past ten when she closed her book, fastened the shutters, and retired.

"I heard her shut the door, and felt quite sure that she had turned the key in the lock."

"The key!" ejaculated Phelps.

"Yes; I had given Miss Harrison instructions to lock the door on the outside and take the key with her when she went to bed. She carried out every one of my injunctions to the letter, and certainly without her co-operation you would not have that paper in your coat-pocket. She departed then and the lights went out, and I was left squatting in the rhododendron-bush.

"The night was fine, but still it was a very weary vigil. Of course it has the sort of excitement about it that the sportsman feels when he lies beside the water-course and waits for the big game. It was very long, though—almost as long, Watson, as when you and I waited in that deadly room when we looked into the little problem of the Speckled Band. There was a church-clock down at Woking which struck the quarters, and I thought more than once that it had stopped. At last, however, about two in the morning, I suddenly heard the gentle sound of a bolt being pushed back and the creaking of a key. A moment later the servants's door was opened, and Mr Joseph Harrison stepped out into the moonlight."

"Joseph!" ejaculated Phelps.

"He was bare-headed, but he had a black coat thrown over his shoulder so that he could conceal his face in an instant if there were any alarm. He walked on tiptoe under the shadow of the wall, and when he reached the window he worked a long-bladed knife through the sash and pushed back the catch. Then he flung open the window, and putting his knife through the crack in the shutters, he thrust the bar up and swung them open.

"From where I lay I had a perfect view of the inside of the room and of every one of his movements. He lit the two candles which stood upon the mantelpiece, and then he proceeded to turn back the corner of the carpet in the neighbourhood of the door. Presently he stooped and picked out a square piece of board, such as is usually left to enable plumbers to get at the joints of the gas-pipes. This one covered, as a matter of fact, the T joint which gives off the pipe which supplies the kitchen underneath. Out of this hiding-place he drew that little cylinder of paper, pushed down the board, rear-ranged the carpet, blew out the candles, and walked straight into my arms as I stood waiting for him outside the window.

"Well, he has rather more viciousness than I gave him credit for, has Master Joseph. He flew at me with his knife, and I had to grass him twice, and got a cut over the knuckles, before I had the upper hand of him. He looked murder out of the only eye he could see with when we had finished, but he listened to reason and gave up the papers. Having got them I let my man go, but I wired full particulars to Forbes this morning. If he is quick enough to catch his bird, well and good. But if, as I shrewdly suspect, he finds the nest empty before he gets there, why, all the better for the govern-ment. I fancy that Lord Holdhurst for one, and Mr Percy Phelps for another, would very much rather that the affair never got as far as a police-court."

"My God!" gasped our client. "Do you tell me that during these long ten weeks of agony the stolen papers were within the very room with me all the time?"

"So it was."

"And Joseph! Joseph a villain and a thief!"

"Hum! I am afraid Joseph's character is a rather deeper and more dangerous one than one might judge from his appearance. From what I have heard from him this morning, I gather that he has lost heavily in dabbling with stocks, and that he is ready to do anything on earth to better his fortunes. Being an absolutely selfish man, when a chance presented itself he did not allow either his sister's happiness or your reputation to hold his hand."

Percy Phelps sank back in his chair.

"My head whirls," said he. "Your words have dazed me."

"The principal difficulty in your case," remarked Holmes, in his didactic fashion, "lay in the fact of there being too much evidence. What was vital was overlaid and hidden by what was irrelevant. Of all the facts which were presented to us we had to pick just those which we deemed to be essential, and then piece them together in their order, so as to reconstruct this very remarkable chain of events. I had already begun to suspect Joseph, from the fact that you had intended to travel home with him that night, and that therefore it was a likely enough thing that he should call for you, knowing the Foreign Office well, upon his way. When I heard that someone had been so anxious to get into the bedroom, in which no one but Joseph could have concealed anything—you told us in your narrative how you had turned Joseph out when you arrived with the doctor—my suspicions all changed to certainties, especially as the attempt was made on the first night upon which the nurse was absent, showing that the intruder was well acquainted with the ways of the house."

"How blind I have been!"

"The facts of the case, as far as I have worked them out, are these: This Joseph Harrison entered the office through the Charles Street door, and knowing his way he walked straight into your room the instant after you left it. Finding no one there he promptly rang the bell, and at the instant that he did so his eyes caught the paper upon the table. A glance showed him that chance had put in his way a State document of immense value, and in an instant he had thrust it into his pocket and was gone. A few minutes elapsed, as you remember, before the sleepy commissionaire drew your attention to the bell, and those were just enough to give the thief time to make his escape.

"He made his way to Woking by the first train, and having examined his booty and assured himself that it really was of immense value, he had concealed it in what he thought was a very safe place, with the intention of taking it out again in a day or two, and carrying it to the French embassy, or wherever he thought that a long price was to be had. Then came your sudden return. He, without a moment's warning, was bundled out of his room, and from that time onward there were always at least two of you there to prevent him from regaining his treasure. The situation to him must have been a maddening one. But at last he thought he saw his chance. He tried to steal in, but was baffled by your wakefulness. You remember that you did not take your usual draught that night."

"I remember."

"I fancy that he had taken steps to make that draught efficacious, and that he quite relied upon your being unconscious. Of course, I understood that he would repeat the attempt whenever it could be done with safety. Your leaving the room gave him the chance he wanted. I kept Miss Harrison in it all day so that he might not anticipate us. Then, having given him the idea that the coast was clear, I kept guard as I have described. I already knew that the papers were probably in the room, but I had no desire to rip up all the planking and skirting in search of them. I let him take them, therefore, from the hiding-place, and so saved myself an infinity of trouble. Is there any other point which I can make clear?"

"Why did he try the window on the first occasion," I asked, "when he might have entered by the door?"

"In reaching the door he would have to pass seven bedrooms. On the other hand, he could get out on to the lawn with ease. Anything else?"

"You do not think," asked Phelps, "that he had any murderous intention? The knife was only meant as a tool."

"It may be so," answered Holmes, shrugging his shoulders. "I can only say for certain that Mr Joseph Harrison is a gentleman to whose mercy I should be extremely unwilling to trust."

43745446R00090

Made in the USA
Middletown, DE
17 May 2017